The Hessian

BOOKS BY HOWARD FAST

THE HESSIAN

A Novel by Howard Fast

William Morrow & Company, Inc., New York 1972

Printed in the United States of America.
Library of Congress Catalog Card Number 76–170236

For Rachel and Jonathan

Contents

The Hessian

1

The Priest

Toward four o'clock of an afternoon in middle May,
the priest appeared, and the following day the whole
thing began. It was the priest who told me about the ship
in the Sound.

The priest came riding up the road from Norwalk on
a donkey—so small a donkey that the rider's feet barely
topped the ground, and the priest was a very small man
indeed, no more than five feet and three inches, about
forty-five years old, with a small protruding belly and a
round moon face, pink and sweaty, from which two
bloodshot and tired pale blue eyes regarded the world
without optimism and yet without despair. It had suddenly turned hot, the first heat of early summer, and
momentarily the glowing new green of springtime seemed
dusty and old. Somewhere the priest had lost his hat, and
the sun was turning his bald head the color of ripe
apples.

Mrs. Feversham and I were in the herb garden, where
I was directing Rodney Stephan how to prune the grape
arbor—not that grapes are anything to speak of in this

wretched Connecticut soil—when I saw the priest and
his donkey top the rise and come down the road toward
the house. My wife pointed toward the manifestation
and wondered what it could be, and I replied that it
appeared to be a priest on a donkey.

"A clergyman?"

"In a manner of speaking. I would guess that this
poor devil is a Roman Catholic priest, and what twist of
fate brought him into this holy nest of Protestantism I
can only guess. In any case, we'll soon find out."

Then I walked through the garden to the road and
waited for him, watching him silently as he brought his
donkey to a halt, climbed out of a makeshift straw
saddle, mopped his brow and wiped his face with a dirty
kerchief, and then crossed himself and muttered a few
words of gratitude, not to me but to God. The blue
eyes then returned my inquiry.

"Feversham?"

"Feversham," I agreed.

"Doctor Feversham?"

"If you will."

"My name is Father Hesselman," he then informed
me, "and I am a Roman Catholic priest—if you will—"
with a slight smile, "and I am very thirsty and my ass
hurts with all the agonies of the damned. Not my
donkey, sir, my ass. I am cursed with boils."

I nodded thoughtfully and understandingly, and my
wife meanwhile, who is less thoughtful and understanding but more practical, sent Rodney to us with a clay
mug of cold water out of the well. It was a full quart
and the priest drained down the whole of it. The little
man was thirsty.

When I had him in my surgery on his belly, washing
his ass with rum and then lancing the boils and drain-

ing them, he explained his hurt when it came to rejection. He was a sensitive little man and was of the stuff that makes poor martyrs, and it made me shudder to think of the pain of sitting day after day on those boils.

"Why the devil did you not go to Doctor Phillips in Norwalk?"

"I went to Doctor Cutler," he answered apologetically.

"Don't wriggle. Cutler could have lanced them."

"He said I was a journeyman from hell. Oh—that one hurt! I think those were his words. He felt that boils were more or less a proper retribution on the part of the Almighty."

"Retribution for what? Don't wriggle," I cautioned him.

"For being a priest."

"What!"

I went deeper in my anger than I had intended, and the poor man whimpered softly.

"Sorry, Father. Did Cutler say that?"

"More or less."

"That filthy, leprous second-rate bastard!"

"That's very hard on him, Mr. Feversham. Consider the man in his surroundings—"

"We will talk about compassion later."

"—and if these are not a sign of God's displeasure—"

"They are most certainly a sign of drinking dirty water and eating bad food. How did you get to me, Father Hesselman?"

"There you are. There is something to speak for Doctor Cutler. He told me there was a Catholic doctor up on the Ridge and he even showed me the road to follow."

"Which opens the gates of heaven, doesn't it? Now listen, Father, can you spend a day or two off the back of your donkey? I have drained the boils and dressed them but they want a bit of coddling."

"I have weak arches," he apologized.

I nodded sympathetically and asked him to stay for dinner. He had a clean cassock with him, and after he had shaved and washed himself, he appeared to be a most pleasant man indeed. He blessed our table and then dug into the roast ham as if he had not eaten in a fortnight. As perhaps he had not.

I had put a good French wine on the table in honor of our guest—the first Catholic priest I had seen in a long, long time—and he drank it with relish and appreciation. It was pleasant to see the little man come to life, praising and admiring all the elements that go to create a little touch of civilization on the Connecticut High Ridge, our silver, our linen, our china, our food; and with his belly full and his soul satisfied, he leaned back and ventured to ask whether I was still a Catholic.

"I should imagine the Holy Father has more important business than my excommunication."

"That's an answer that is no answer."

"Well, sir, Father Hesselman," I said, "I have not made my confession for more than five years, I have not prayed with a pure heart, I have hated and not admonished myself not to hate, and of course I have not set foot in a Catholic church for quite a while. I am married to a Protestant woman"—I nodded toward my wife —"withal a lovely one, but I coddle my conscience by never setting foot in a Protestant church either. For three years I led a regiment against the British, not because I love the colonies but because I hate the damned English, who put my father to death for no other reason than that he was a Catholic; so if I were bored as hell with being a Catholic for any other and every other reason, I would remain one because the British are not. There's your answer."

"It's exceedingly complex and I am not sure that I follow it entirely," Father Hesselman said.

"I suppose so."

"It is the manner of being a doctor," my wife, Alice, put in. "Brusque but kindly. It has become a habit with him."

"Not kindly," I said sharply.

"Why did you leave the army?" the priest asked me. "Have you soured?"

"Have you?" I answered with annoyance. "Or are you some damn Tory?"

"Evan!" my wife cried.

Father Hesselman regarded me without rancor and gave me to understand that his church had been used as a hospital for over three years now.

"Then I am sorry, sir. Forgive me."

The priest smiled, and I realized that the half bottle of wine had made him pleasantly relaxed and moderately drunk.

"Where is your church?" I asked him.

"In Baltimore, where a Catholic is hardly less common than a Protestant."

"And where are you bound for, if I may ask?"

"Rhode Island, where nine Catholic families asked that a priest be sent to them, and thus my fortune and perhaps their misfortune."

"Why never," said Alice. "I consider them fortunate indeed."

"May they consider themselves thus, dear lady," Father Hesselman replied.

"But why are you here on the Ridge? Why didn't you take ship and save yourself the misery of that stupid beast you ride?"

"My donkey and I are fond of each other. I try to be less a burden and more a companion."

"That's a beast that not even a saint could love."

"You are being utterly impossible," my wife said to me. "What will the good father think?"

"I can damn well guess what he thinks. Put him down in this nest of long-nosed righteousness, and he will think likewise. As I do. Meanwhile, he regards me as an insolent, vulgar, irascible and godless man, and perhaps he is right. I soured," I told the priest, "but that isn't why I am here. Have I not right to be here? I'm a physician, and work at my trade. I took a shot in my leg and I walk with a gimp, as you may have noticed."

"I noticed," the priest said sadly.

"Evan, Evan," said Alice, "we sit at dinner and not at a committee meeting."

"And if you came up from New York," I demanded of the priest, "why did you not take passage on some packet?"

"There's a British frigate in the Sound."

"Hah!"

"I saw it with my own eyes, Doctor Feversham."

"Where?"

"At anchor off the rivermouth. What do you people call it now? Salituk?"

"Saugatuck."

"Right. There she was, with ship's boats going back and forth. They were slaughtering meat. Soldiers standing all around and keeping guard."

"Redcoats?"

"No—oh, no."

"How near were you?"

"On the King's road—maybe two hundred paces away. But my eyes are good. Soldiers in green coats with yellow facings. Black boots, white kneebreeches—"

"Yes, Hessians." I added as kindly as I could, "I am not really interested in Hessians, Father Hesselman, or in the war which should be done with and drags on and on and on—and I asked you how you came up onto the Ridge by donkey seat, and you told me."

He was a bit hurt and I suppose he felt somewhat rejected, and my wife looked at me accusingly; but the little man took heart from some clotted cream custard and good coffee and asked me, withal diffidently, in what I truly was interested.

"My immortal soul, if I have one."

He reassured me.

"You're a damn pleasant chap," I told him, "and here I have done nothing but insult you and use my own bad manners to pin you up against your good nature."

"Not at all," he protested. "Not even the father of the prodigal son could have been more kindly, for you healed my wounds and comforted me and fed me food and will give me bed, so believe me, I pray for you in return for the love and kindness from you and your good lady."

I woke the following morning half an hour before the sunrise and went looking for the priest. He was praying at the little fountain in the garden; and then we both sat there on the wooden bench and he heard my confession. With daylight, he was on his way, clutching a basket of bread and meat that Alice gave him, bouncing on the donkey's back and undoing all the good I had done for those boils of his.

He came in and out of my life, for I never saw Father

Hesselman again—yet in a way he was a catalyst for me, and through all the terrible business that followed, I could not get him and his foolish, gentle little smile out of my head. And, of course, he brought me news of the British frigate in the Sound.

It was out of that ship the Hessian detachment came, and why they had to make their way the fifteen miles up onto the Ridge, I will never know. If I could make this up as a story, it would be of one piece, but in its truth it is full of gaps, holes, questions asked and left unanswered. Like most of the folk on the Ridge, I pieced the tale together even though, as you will see, I was privy to more of it than anyone else, and some of it was of my own cause.

For one thing, it was I who insisted to Jenny Perkins, who was schoolteacher over at Ridgefield, that Saul Clamberham could learn. He had come into her school towering over the kids there, and while some of them knew him and realized that he was harmless, others were terrified of the great, oversized halfwit with his loose, slobbering speech.

I said, let him go to the school and sit in back and learn—I said that, when they brought the matter to me, as if Saul's sickness were something I could diagnose and cure. "He wants to learn. It's a human right. God gave us minds and put us on earth to learn. He's not mindless, only addled, and what harm does he do if he sits quietly in back of the school?"

"My school?" Miss Perkins exclaimed.

"Not yours, not mine, Miss Perkins. A school is like a church, Miss Perkins. How can you lay claim to it?"

"I lay claim to the right to teach. How can I teach with Saul Clamberham there? He's a grotesque. He's a mindless idiot. Anyway, the children are afraid of him.

Have they no rights? Is a school not for the children?"

Squire Abraham Hunt had come with her. What did I have against Squire Hunt, except my own petulance at the sort of a man he was? He was a commanding man, and I suppose I don't like commanding men who know precisely what is right and what is wrong. He was a patriot and I was a soldier and a surgeon and a patriot only by the most objective of definitions. He made decisions and acted upon them, and I lived under the lurking suspicion that decisions—or at least most of them—were for God and not for men. His decision was that a physician should examine Saul Clamberham and bundle him off to the madhouse in Boston, which was the only reason he sought me out; and I can imagine what a cursed fate upon Ridgefield he felt it was to have no doctor of their own, that is, no Protestant doctor to save them from the healing of a devilish Papist.

"He's harmless," I said. "Isn't life stinking hard enough without showing our purposefulness against a poor damn halfwit?"

"Then must I close up school?" Miss Perkins demanded.

"No, I don't think so. What does Saul want?"

"To read. He desires to read the Book. The Bible, to make it plain to you, Mr. Feversham."

"I am aware that the Bible is called the Book, Miss Perkins, being not entirely damned by my Catholic ignorance."

"We can do without impertinence," Squire Hunt said shortly.

"And now you teach me manners. I thank you. He will not learn to read, Miss Perkins, not ever, but I think he could learn small counting. Certainly to addition of one and two and three. If you give me just five or ten minutes after school, I will see to it that he does not interrupt classes."

"And why not give him the lessons yourself, Colonel"—he enjoyed using my military title because he knew I had cast it away—"since you regard him with such affection?"

"I would indeed and so would my wife, but he would have no faith in what transpired outside of the schoolhouse. If Miss Perkins supplies him with an old piece of broken slate and a bit of chalk, he will be no more a nuisance."

And she agreed, and that is how Saul Clamberham came to his bit of broken slate and his small addition. So there was the priest and the British frigate in the Sound and Saul Clamberham, whose mind was addled, but so without hate or resentment or gall that sometimes I felt he had the better of all of us. That's how it began.

2

The Hessians

RAYMOND HEATHER'S FATHER was one of those Quakers who had fled Massachusetts for the religious security of Rhode Island, and when Raymond took him a wife, he came down onto the Ridge where he bought a freehold on half a hundred acres of rocky ground. He had been there seventeen years, cobbling shoes in the wintertime and raising sheep in the summertime, but he was still a stranger, a recipient of the dubious and grudging grace that Connecticut extended to Quakers, Papists, Jews and others of the damned. He had grown, meanwhile, numerous sheep, a daughter of sixteen named Sally, a boy of twelve who bore the name of Jacob, Annie of four years and a toddler of twelve months named Joanna. He had a strong, cheerful wife, Sarah, who had been an Otis in Boston; and that helped not only to cheer his life but to give him some small standing with the local bigots. He was one of my first patients when I took up my practice after being mustered out, and since he knew the game of chess—withal a bad player—we spent an occasional winter evening together.

It was his boy, Jacob Heather, who saw what happened between the halfwit, Saul Clamberham, and the Hessians; and except for Hans Pohl, he was the only witness. But nothing Hans Pohl said afterwards contradicted Jacob's story, and there was no reason to disbelieve anything the boy said.

The Hessian detachment was landed from the frigate; there is no doubt about that; plenty of witnesses to the landing, and the uniforms they wore matched the priest's description. Why two squads of them—sixteen men in all and drummer boy and officer—were selected to march up onto the High Ridge, I do not know; but someone offered the explanation that another British warship had sailed up the Hudson River, and perhaps the Hessians were sent to sight it or communicate with it, since there are places on the High Ridge where one can see the Hudson River and Long Island Sound from the same spot.

Believe me, there are no better soldiers in the King's army than the Hessians and it was no great risk for them to come up onto the Ridge with sixteen muskets. Their first day's march—on the same day that the priest spent at my house—was made quietly and carefully, wide of the Post Road to Danbury, mostly along the old Indian trail, I suppose, and they camped for the night somewhere on the Saugatuck River. No one saw them that day, or if anyone did, they kept quiet about it and about why they sounded no warning. No one in his right mind wants war in his back yard, and since the war was down in Virginia now, only a damn fool would take any measures to introduce it into Connecticut. It was different four years ago, but by now everyone had a bellyful of the killing and the burning and the accusing, and there was a sort of understanding to the effect of live and let live.

So no one bothered the Hessians or spoke of them, and perhaps even Jacob Heather would have looked at them as pretty toy soldiers if the thing had not happened right under his nose. He had gone out to fish before the sunrise, and climbing over Hightop with the sun bursting out of the east, he saw the Hessians below him, coming up the trail from the creek, with Saul Clamberham among them and a rope around Saul's neck. With that, the Heather boy went down into the new fern and dry leaves, watching with only his eyes and nose to show, and then it happened, no more than fifty yards from where he lay.

They hanged Saul Clamberham.

Night and day meant little to Saul Clamberham; he had no home, no place, no kith or kin, and sometimes he slept in the Quaker meetinghouse, and sometimes on a cold night he would find a corner of someone's hearth, for he was gentle and unoffensive and would curl up like a big dog and demand no more than a dog would, or again on a warm day, as this mid-May was, he would bed down in the grass or on a pile of dead leaves in the woods. So he must have done, and the beat of the Hessian drum, calling the men to order, probably awakened him. He had the piece of slate that Miss Perkins had given him and a butt of chalk, and he decided to make a counting game with the Hessians.

They began their march, and he walked parallel to them through the woods, trying to mark their numbers on the slate. Heaven only knows what he put down on the slate, what marks, what gibberish! It was a game to him, and he pretended to stalk them. Perhaps he knew that they could see him, for the woods are open in May, and perhaps he felt secure in his mindless world, for everyone knew that he was a halfwit and the worst he ever got was a blow across the head or the back. In any case, they saw him, and the Hessian commander, Captain Wolfgang Hauser, told his sergeant to count a thousand paces and then tell off a detail to take the spy. He was only that to them, a spy, and they took him without any trouble. He didn't even try to run away, just stood there grinning at them, and when they examined the slate, he nodded proudly.

I imagine that they suspected something wrong about him, his loose lips, his shambling walk, his bare feet and the old cast-off clothes; but in war men are not normal men and they do not think or react as normal men do. They are drawn tight and full of fear and anger, and this was a detachment of men in enemy country. Still, in all fairness to the Hessian officer, Hauser, he did not react at once but put a rope around Saul's neck and led him on for another two miles while he turned the matter over in his mind. Hans Pohl, the drummer boy, said afterwards that he felt the decision the captain was coming to and it made him sick at heart to think about it, and possibly others felt it too and had the same reaction. During the two miles, Captain Hauser came to the decision that Saul Clamberham was a spy and that he must hang him. Then they were just below Hightop, where Jacob Heather lay hidden.

Hauser drew up his horse in front of a tree, and then said flatly to his sergeant:

"This will do. Hang him to this tree," pointing to a great spreading ash which loomed over the road at that point. "Throw the rope over a limb and be done with it."

He spoke in German, but when the sergeant threw the rope over a limb, Saul realized what they were up to, and he began to blubber and went down on his knees.

He pleaded for his life as best he could, while the sergeant tried to explain in broken English that Saul was a spy, and that a spy must die, and that it was perfectly legal according to the articles of war.

Hauser sat on his horse, patient, formal and attempting to be very correct. Afterwards, I asked Jacob whether Hauser appeared to be angry, and the boy answered that he didn't think so. I suppose I have spent some futile hours brooding over the kind of a man Hauser must have been, a well-trained, efficient soldier, very much by the book and without a great deal of imagination. We discovered later that he had a wife and three children at home in Germany, and I saw an unfinished letter to them, full of sentiment and homesickness. But sentiment has little to do with practicality. The Hessian had a prisoner whom he could not release and who would incommode his march, and within his training there was a solution. The sergeant detailed four men to drag the rope, and the captain ordered Hans Pohl to beat a roll.

"God have mercy on your soul," the captain said.

Then the four men walked the rope away, and Saul Clamberham was hoisted up into the air, where he strangled to death.

It was not a pretty sight for a twelve-year-old boy to see, and Jacob Heather lay frozen in his bed of leaf and fern until the Hessians marched away, leaving poor Saul's body swaying from the tree.

3

The Ambush

WHEN THE HESSIANS had marched away and out of sight, Jacob Heather began to cry. There was Saul Clamberham's body swaying slightly in the soft wind, and the boy just lay there looking at it and crying. It was the first time he had ever seen anybody put to death or killed in any fashion whatsoever, and it was the most awful thing he had ever witnessed. Yet he managed to get up enough courage to go down into the valley and touch the body.

"Saul Clamberham!" he called out, not being able to establish the finality of death either on the corpse or in his own mind. He could reach up as high as Saul's bare foot, and he pinched the foot to elicit some response from Saul. It was then that the full immensity of death overwhelmed him and terror took hold of him.

He ran away. Pausing to sob for his breath now and then, he ran the full two and a half miles to the village.

It was the same morning, as I said, that I bade Father Hesselman good-bye; and then I mounted my horse and rode off to the village to pick up a post I was expecting, occupying myself along the way with regrets for the churlishness of my manner toward the gentle little priest and for the paucity and dishonesty of my confession. It was true that in the act of confession, I forgot the most important things, but that was no consolation. The fact was that I remembered them now.

The post-station was at the inn, and it was just after nine o'clock in the morning that I arrived there to discover that the post from Norwalk held nothing for me. I went into the taproom then for small beer to wash my throat, and there was Abraham Hunt, sitting behind the big common table and holding his morning magistracy.

There was never love lost between Hunt and myself, not from the first day I bought property on the Ridge, and my being a Catholic and an Englishman is less of a reason for his attitude than a hook to hang it onto. We agree only on a certain amount of respect, and for whatever I hold against him, as a magistrate he is fair and objective. He was in the process, that morning, of fining Salem Alan five dollars silver for poaching Isaac Leeds' land, and Salem Alan was his friend and cousin, while Isaac Leeds had as little use for Hunt as any of the Leeds clan over on Redding Ridge. Alan blew his temper, and Hunt roared at him, very conscious of my presence:

"God damn you, Salem—you talk like that in my court and I'll break your back and do it with my own two hands!"

He could have, too. Abraham Hunt weighed sixteen stone, and most of it bone and muscle, a pair of enormous shoulders, with a long, slope-jawed head on a neck as thick as my thigh.

"How are you going to prove I poached him?" Salem Alan demanded. "Where's a skin or carcass?"

"You're a poacher," Hunt said with finality. "You're the worst damn poacher on the Ridge."

"So anyone accuses me of poaching—"

"Not anyone," Leeds interrupted. "Myself."

"You got your judgment, sir," Hunt said. "This is a fair court. Colonel Feversham stands there, drinking his small beer like the fine British gentry he is, and comparing. Comparing, Brother Leeds. Will you have him think us worse savages than he does?"

"I think you the soul of gentility, Squire Hunt," I said quietly. "On my soul."

"On your Catholic soul?"

"No doubt, no doubt," I answered amiably. Whatever he was after I did not want it that morning, and perhaps my confession was more effective than I had imagined. Whether it would have led to any more, with Hunt's truculence, I do not know, for at that moment Jacob Heather burst into the inn, weeping and sobbing and trying to speak and unable to speak. There were half a dozen men in the taproom and half a dozen kids who had picked up Jacob on their way to school—where he should have been—so it made for quite a crowd.

The boy saw me and buried his face in my coat; and for the moment I thought it was only the other boys after him to give him more of the endless bullying that specified his being of the Company of Friends and therefore sinfully different from themselves. I gave Jacob the comfort of my bulk and shot out an accusing finger at the children.

"If this is any more of your damned bullying—"

"Never laid a finger on him, Mr. Feversham."

"Swear it!"

"God's honor!"

"He came running like the devil was after him."

His spasmodic sobs were easing now, and I held him away from me, asking him, "What is it, Jacob? What is it?"

Then he managed to get the words out. "Saul Clamberham is dead." Not understandable at first. The men, the boys—they were curious now, pressing around him. I gave him a taste of my small beer, and then he managed:

"Saul Clamberham is dead."

"Where? How? Speak up now, boy!" Hunt cried, taking command of the situation as he always did. "Stop that blubbering."

"His breath is wasted. Damn you, Hunt, can't you see his breath is wasted? Give the boy a chance."

Then we waited while Jacob's chest stopped heaving, until at last he was able to say, "Hanged. Hanged up on a tree."

"Who?"

"Saul Clamberham."

"Well, what's he saying?" came the demands from those in back. "Who was hanged?"

"Saul Clamberham!" someone shouted.

"Speak up!" Hunt said more gently. "Speak up, boy. Tell us what happened."

"The Hessians caught Saul Clamberham and hanged him."

"The boy is a liar," from the back.

From the back, too, the voice of Miss Perkins, "Oh, this is very fine indeed, a whole school of children in the devil's bedroom, oh, yes, very fine indeed."

"Jacob, Jacob," Hunt said, shaking the boy slightly, getting down on one knee to his size, "Jacob, what did you see? There be no Hessians on the Ridge or in all Connecticut for that matter."

"I saw them," the boy insisted, crying normally now. "I saw them hang Saul Clamberham."

"Where?"

"Hightop track, on the big ash."

"No Hessians," someone kept repeating from the back, and someone else explained to Miss Perkins that a young liar needed a good sound thrashing and would lie no more.

"Where would Hessians come from, boy?"

"He's not lying," I said. "There's a British warship off the Saugatuck across the islands, and they landed Hessians."

"How do you know?" Hunt demanded.

"A priest stopped by for the night. He saw them."

Cold silence then.

"A Catholic priest," I said, and then I asked Jacob, "What color did they wear?"

"Green coats with yellow. Big hats."

"They're the Jager Regiment," I said. "Why don't you listen to the boy?"

"All right, Jacob," Hunt said, his voice changing, his voice flat and dry. "Where were you when you saw them?"

"Like I told thee, I lay on Hightop."

"Did you count them?"

"Yes."

"How many?"

"Sixteen and a drummer boy and one of them on a horse."

"The others on foot?"

"Yes, sir."

"All right," Hunt said again, and stood up and said

to Salem Alan, "Muster the militia. I want at least thirty men and I want them mounted and I want them an hour from now, no longer. Do you understand?"

"Where at, Squire?"

"At Naham Buskin's place. And tell them to load with heavy birdshot for close range." He turned to me. "Will you go to Hightop, Feversham? It's one thing to hang a man properly—the poor bastard could still be alive."

I nodded.

We left the others there at the inn, and mounted and rode to Hightop. There's no proper cart track into the place, only the old Indian trail, but we rode hard and reached the big ash in no more than twenty minutes, and there was Saul Clamberham's body swaying in the shining, feathery new leaves of the big ash.

"He's dead," I said. I knew it without touching him. His neck was broken, his face swollen and purple, and then I dismounted and felt his body; it was cold already with rigor mortis hardening his limbs. I took out my pocketknife.

"What are you going to do?" Hunt demanded.

"Cut him down."

"If we lay him in the woods, the animals will be at him in no time."

"We'll take him to Buskin's place. It's only a couple of miles."

"There's no time."

"There's time enough, Hunt. You can't let him hang there like that."

"There's no time. Understand me, Feversham—those Hessians are not going back to their ship."

"Why not?"

"Because I'm going to stop them."

"With the militia? Hunt, you're not serious."

"I've never been more serious in my life. Where do you think they went?"

"To the High Ridge—where else?"

"Where else? They want to see the river, but they won't stay there—not sixteen of them. They'll be down, and they won't stop marching until they reach the Sound."

"That's only a guess."

"What in hell's wrong with you, Feversham?" he said heatedly. "You know damn well it's no guess—because there's nothing else for them to do. They've hanged a man—our man. They're in our country, up here on the Ridge where they couldn't raise a corporal's guard to lift a finger for them, and until they get out of here they won't rest."

"Maybe they're out of here already."

He leaned over and pointed to the tracks in the soft spring mud.

"And if they come back another way?"

"What other way? On King's Highway? On the Post Road? They're not that stupid. They're on the old trail because they have a map and they know the country, and they'll come back the same way. What is it, Feversham— are you afraid of them?"

I cut the rope now, lowering Saul's body to the ground before I answered him, nor did I lose my temper but said quite flatly, "If you want it that way, Squire, I am afraid—yes. I have lived through seventeen battles in my lifetime, France, Spain—and here too, and I have been afraid every time. This war is over, Squire—you know that as well as I do, and they're beaten, and you know that as well as I do; but these German men are still the best soldiers in the world, and I say let them go, let them get back on their lousy ship and sail away, and then perhaps we live the way God meant us to."

"Will you read me God's word, Feversham? I'll read you some—an eye for an eye and a tooth for a tooth."

"Saul's dead. Let him rest. Let it finish. We need no more dead." I tried to lift Saul's body, but he had been a big man and his body was more than I could manage alone.

"Let go of him," Hunt said, shouldering me aside, and then he bent over the body and lifted it and set it across the saddle of his horse in one easy motion. "Mount your horse, Colonel," he told me magnanimously, "and I'll lead mine. You're right. We have time to lay Saul out in a Christian manner and meet the Hessians too."

There was no use in arguing with him, and he was not to be shaken by reason or mercy but wholly directed to the simple fact of revenge. There are times when the circumstances of life become implacable, and then you have the feeling that no force or argument or plea can alter them, one event moving in the tracks of another with the mindless, plodding motion of a great ox; and so I felt then, and we went on in silence to Naham Buskin's farm. His outlying field sloped up to the Indian track and shielded itself behind a long stone wall, and as we went along the wall, the ground falling away and invisible on the other side, I saw immediately what was in Abraham Hunt's mind, and had to admire the man for his scope and imagination—and I saw him as not so unlike myself, one man sitting inside the other, like six lonely brothers in a single shell, six minds and wills tearing at the huge, deceptive bulk of Abraham Hunt.

Buskin had a large landhold, almost two hundred acres, which had been part of Lord Denny's grant and under litigation for the past twenty years. Through all the years of the litigation, Squire Hunt had held Buskin's ground rents in escrow, and since Lord Denny never chose to visit his holdings in America, the money was not claimed and the litigation wore on. When the war came, the Connecticut House turned Denny's land over to his tenants, and the good citizens of New Haven tarred and feathered Lord Denny's lawyer, who subsequently fled to Canada. Squire Hunt then turned over to Naham Buskin six hundred pounds of hard British money, which not only made Naham one of the rich men of the county but placed him completely in a debt of gratitude to Hunt.

So there was no question now about Buskin's willingness to use his place as a rallying point, and as we rode past the stone wall and down the hill and up on over another hill to the house, we saw the militiamen coming in by ones and twos, and already a cluster of them dismounted, slaking their thirst at Buskin's well. They rode through the new grass of Buskin's pastures, framed by the new May leafing, and they made a lovely, almost fanciful picture from the distance. By the time we reached them, there were thirty-two present, and during the next few minutes four more rode in. Buskin's family came out to join the excitement. He had three married daughters and eleven grandchildren out of them, a great crowd of excited kids; and of course the sons-in-law and Buskin himself would have it no other way than to join us. There was no greater patriot than Buskin on all the Ridge—and with reason.

Abraham Hunt climbed onto the well-housing and told the men, gathered close around him, what he intended to do. I heard it out of one ear, for events were moving fast and I was making my arrangements with Mrs.

Buskin for bandages and for some sharp knives that I could use for instruments—since mine were home and not to be gotten in time—scissors, and the biggest needles she had and clean linen thread and rum and some tin basins and a small saw.

Meanwhile, Hunt laid out his plan. It was simple and direct. The men would leave their horses at Buskin's place, go on the double across to the end pasture and take their places behind the stone wall. They would box the two ends of the Hessian column with their fire and make an ambush from which there was no escape. The plan was simple, direct, practical and brutal, and in less time than it takes to put this down, the whole lot of them were running behind Hunt, hot on the trail and afraid now that they would miss the game.

I took a few minutes more to complete my supplies, and then I followed but not running, and when Hunt saw me coming up the slope he waved frantically for me to get down. When I reached him, he was coldly angry.

"Suppose they come on now," he said. "You would have blown it, Feversham."

"I can't run, Squire," I explained, "and I can't walk bent over. And since a Hessian bullet did it, it would make for a certain poetic justice, wouldn't it?"

"Damned if I see that."

I chose a spot between two of the militiamen and laid out my hastily gathered collection of makeshift bandages and surgical instruments against the wall. The men were glad to see me, and while they were grinning and swearing softly in their best manner and making whatever crude jokes they could think of, they did not share Hunt's absolute and unshaken resolve and confidence. While the sight of a doctor, even with the crude tools

I had gathered from Mrs. Buskin, directed their attention to the fact of mortality, it also reassured them. There were thirty-seven of them against the sixteen or seventeen Hessians, but to most of them that did not even the odds. They were farmers, storekeepers, a blacksmith and his two helpers, two carpenters and a cooper, and Biddle, the fuller, and Saxon, the undertaker, who was past sixty. The youngest in the group was fourteen, and the oldest was ninety-one.

Hessian, on the other hand, was not a name for men but for a nightmare that had lived with us so long that it had become part of our language and culture, men of steel will and determination, men trained to be machines; and I suppose there was no one in that line behind the stone wall who did not somehow believe that the Hessians could destroy them, ambush or not. To their credit, they stayed there—or to the credit of the will of Hunt, who now walked along their ranks, telling them to shut up and pray if they must but pray silently, and not one blessed word did he want out of them, not a word, not a question, not a sneeze.

"Good heavens, Abraham," Saxon said, "it may be hours."

"Then be it hours, and that's the last thing said by any of you. You'll stay down behind that wall and hugging that wall until I give the signal"—he hooked his pinkies in his lips and whistled softly—"that signal, and then you up and fire. It's the first fire that counts, but once you fire, reload and don't think of one damn thing but that, reload, and if you get to reload and you're still alive and whole, get up and fire at anything moving in that road, but just remember that it's the first fire that counts and if you blow that, God help you! I want the ten men at each end to box it—to kill the leaders and the trailers—and the rest of you shoot at whatever is right in front of you. And aim—don't just blow your piece. Aim. You all got scattershot, so aim on the shoulder halfway to the elbow, and then if you pull your gun, you'll still have your target. Over-prime your pieces, and if you don't spark, keep your head and cock and shoot again. That's it."

Silence then—no sound but the breathing and an occasional rustle or crunch as one of the men shifted his position. Stooping below the wall, Hunt came over to me and said half mockingly, "Well, surgeon—ready?"

I was sprawled at the base of the wall, as comfortable as I could make myself. I looked at Hunt without answering him.

"Feversham," he said, "one day, you and me, we'll have a long talk and get out all the worms that are eating us. If there's nothing else about you I like, you've got guts."

Still I didn't answer, for it was too late to talk any more about the madness of the horror he contemplated. So a man moves with a thing and surrenders his mind and his honor. Hunt was wrong. I had no guts. I knew too much about war, and Hunt knew too little.

For a full half hour we lay there and nothing happened. Hunt had warned Mrs. Buskin to keep her children in the house, and when I left she was already chasing the yelling, protesting brats indoors. I regretted now that I had not had enough presence of mind to get our men to bring along a few buckets, for when you can't wash a bleeding wound the work is twice as difficult; yet I knew that Hunt would raise all kinds of hell if I even suggested that we send a man back for water.

The thought of water made me realize how dry the men were, how dry their lips which they licked constantly, how dry their inner being, while their hands were wet with nervousness—constantly rubbing their hands on their breeches—and sweat beaded their brows and wet their clothes. Yet they remained quiet, and if words were spoken, the whispers were so soft I heard them not at all. It was not that they were afraid of Abraham Hunt, at least not consciously afraid, but Hunt dominated them as he had for all of his adult life, for he had been magistrate over them for twenty years; and their obedience to Hunt was a matter of habit. The meadow and woods life around us relaxed as the men remained still and silent; the robins came close and the bluejays waxed bold. A snake slithered in and out of the stone wall and a chipmunk perched upon it and regarded us, and over us the May wind blew and the lovely new foliage rustled and fluttered with the excitement of spring.

And then we heard the drum.

The drum was the signature of the Hessians, and when I heard it my scalp stiffened and a cold chill raised gooseflesh on my bare arms. The drum defined the Hessians. There they were, in the midst of enemy country, a good fifteen miles from the ship which had brought them and which represented the only real security they could look to. They were sixteen and a drummer boy and an officer, and already they had hanged a man of the neighborhood, yet such was their confidence in themselves as trained and disciplined soldiers and their contempt for the Yankee farmers of Connecticut, that they would not still their voice. The drum was their presence, like the rattles on the tail of a snake that is feared by creatures with a hundred times its strength; the drum said, here we are and be damned to you! Leave us alone!

We did not see them come. As I looked down the line
of our men, each of them crouched on one knee behind
the wall, it seemed to me that they were frozen in a kind
of terror from which they would not be released—all
of them but Hunt, who caught my eye and nodded with
cool deliberation.

The drumbeat approached, a steady marching beat,
tad-tad-dum-dum-dum, tad-tad-dum-dum-dum, over and
over, and now we could hear the sound of their boots,
and the picture was clear in my mind's eye, the drummer
boy out in front, the officer on his horse, the men following, two by two, their shining black hats swaying with
their step, their greased pigtails standing out sharp in
back, the green jackets, the bright yellow facings, the
bayonet scabbards slapping their thighs, the big, waxed
mustaches they sported—all of it dredged out of my
memory as a signature to screaming death. And then
the drumbeat was in front of us, so close we could almost
feel the sound vibrating in the air, and through cracks
in the wall I could see the drummer boy's boots. I
glanced at Hunt.

He was in the act of putting his fingers into his mouth,
and an instant later, his piercing whistle cut the air, and
the militiamen behind the wall stood up and fired their
guns—all of them except the Cutler twins, fourteen
years old, who remained under the wall, frozen stiff
with fear.

I stood up with them, and in that moment of con-
fused, exploded sight—which is all one ever has at the
joining of battle—I saw the Hessian detachment cut
down and destroyed. I think they died with that first
volley. The militiamen had loaded heavily, with double
and triple charges of birdshot and powder, and shooting
point-blank at targets only a few feet away, they could

not miss. In his arrogance, the Hessian captain did not even put out a point man. His head was blown open and another shot tore his horse's throat, yet it leaped the wall, dragging the officer's body by a stirrup, and then it rolled over dead in the meadow. The others died in the road. They lay there, some of them twisting and screaming, but most of them dead instantly, yet our men were reloading like mad and firing again and again. Powder smoke began to blanket the road, and then they fired into the smoke, and all the time they were screaming and yelling, their screaming mounting in intensity as the sounds from the Hessians died away.

I yelled at Hunt, "Stop the fire! Stop it! It's over!"

But no one heard me. I limped across to Hunt as fast as my bad leg would take me, and he was loading his gun again and I shouted into his face, "Hunt, for God's sake, stop it! Some of them may be left alive! It's murder now!"

He never heard me. He was looking past me, across the meadow, and in spite of myself I followed his eyes, and there, on the other side of the meadow, where it sloped up again onto a high hill, a Hessian was running. It was the drummer boy, his drum still strapped to his shoulder and swinging wildly behind him. Already, he was well out of musket-shot. He paused for a moment, looked back, unhooked his drum and flung it away, and then raced on into the woods on the ridge.

4

The Chase

THE HESSIANS lay in the narrow Indian track, except for
their captain, who was dead with his horse in the
meadow, half his head blown away. I have seen places
of death, but this was in a way more terrible than any
I had ever looked at before, and when I walked among
the bodies, the blood rose up over my toes, splashed from
under my boots and made a ghastly sucking noise with
each step. The narrow ditch of the trail was still acrid
with the smell of gunsmoke, but there was no sound.
Even Abraham Hunt held his peace, and the militiamen
stood in horrified silence—the wild thing of fear and
hate gone out of them—staring at what they had wrought.
No one of them moved to come after me, and as I
turned body after body, here a man of middle years,
here a boy, here a blue-eyed, yellow-haired youth in the
fullness of his young manhood, no one of the militiamen
stepped forward to help me; as perhaps, God help them,
they could not.

Suddenly, one of the Hessians lurched to his feet,
blood running from his mouth and nose, stood swaying

a moment, and then fell back—dead when I reached
him. One of the Cutler twins cried out in surprise, and
Oscar Latham, our fat innkeeper who had never seen
such a sight as this before in his life, began to blubber
like a child. Then most of the others turned away because they could look no longer, and then I found a
Hessian still alive.

"For Christ's sake," I cried out, "one of you bring
my kit and bandages!"

Hunt brought them to me. "He's alive?"

"Alive," I said shortly, tearing the man's jacket apart.
He opened his eyes then and looked at me, wet brown
eyes, like a deer's eyes.

"Save him, Feversham," Hunt begged me.

"So you can hang him?"

"You bastard."

"Give me bandage and shut up! Send someone for
water! Water—do you hear me?"

The other Cutler twin came through the carnage with
a canteen, but it was no use. There were twenty birdshot wounds in the poor devil's body and a gaping hole
in his stomach. He died as I tried to close up the hole
over his bare gut. I went from body to body, sixteen
men in a little river of their blood, playing my own
game and understanding full well Hunt's plea, and pleading myself, "Pray God Almighty, let one of them be
alive and live!"—the first time I had asked God for anything in a long while, and this time for the impossible
gift of life where there was no life. They had been
blasted into death. They lay in that strange disorder of
the violently destroyed, this one flung into the brush,
that one with arms and legs wildly askew, this one hud-
dled over like a child in a womb, that one with arms

outstretched, this one without a hand, that one without a face—I had to touch them and move them all, every one of them, holding wrists still warm and begging for a pulse, wiping away the blood so that I could lift the lid of an eye and see it remain open. And then it was done.

"All dead?" Hunt asked, his voice muted.

The militiamen were gathering. They walked gingerly into the blood. After the first reaction, the dead are hardly to be feared as much as the living. Some of them took off their shoes. Blood washes easier from bare feet than from leather.

"All dead, Squire Hunt, all dead," I replied.

"They're soldiers, Feversham."

"Dead soldiers."

"They're soldiers. They came into our land. They hanged Saul Clamberham. They murdered."

"What difference does that make now, Squire? They're dead."

"The officer's in the field with the horse."

I walked away from him then, climbed over Buskin's wall, and went to the officer. I said before that in my time I have seen some things, but the sight of the Hessian officer lying there with the brains pouring from his open head was more than I could take, and I began to vomit. Coughing and gasping, I came out of it to see Hunt there, watching me.

"We'll have to bury the horse," he said, and then he walked over to the Hessian officer and stared at him for a long moment.

"Do you know the insignia, Feversham?" he asked, without looking at me.

"He's a captain. It's a forester regiment. They call them Jagers. They're very good."

"Not good enough. You know one of them got away?"

"The drummer boy."

Hunt was bending over the officer, going through his pockets. He came up with a wallet, which he opened and riffled through. Then he glanced up to see me watching him.

"I'm not robbing the dead, Feversham."

"I didn't think you were."

"No one's robbing the dead, Feversham. I made that plain, and that I'd break the back of anyone who did."

"That's one small comfort."

"What eats at you, Feversham? You were a soldier, I was a soldier. When we fought the big battle on the other side of Ridgefield, there were ten times that many dead, and not Germans either but our own kids. You want me to weep for them?"

"No. That would be useless, wouldn't it?"

"It damn well would," he agreed, continuing to search the wallet. "Can you read German, Feversham?"

"A little."

"Try this," handing me a letter.

The script was beautifully controlled, each word a small work of penmanship art. There were many words I did not understand, but I could read enough of it to get the drift.

"Squire! Squire!" Isaac Leeds was calling. "Where do you want the rings and money?"

"Lay it out against the wall. I want sixteen packets, and so help me God, if one of you takes a penny out of it, I'll see him in hell!"

"They're all wearing gold rings—every mother's son of them."

"Then there'll be sixteen gold rings, so help me!"

"And then what do you do with it?" I asked him.

"Can you read the letter?"

Naham Buskin joined us. "Squire—you can't bury them here. My goodness, I'll never sleep a night through again if you bury them here."

"Did you intend to bury them here?" I demanded of Hunt.

He was uneasy at this. "If I did?"

"My God, man, they're Christian."

"Old man Biddle is sick," someone said, the group around the dead officer growing but keeping their faces averted. "He's vomiting out his guts, Doctor. He's taking a fit and he's beginning to get the shakes."

"Give him a drink of water."

"Now, Feversham," Hunt said, "you're giving me moral readings, is that it?"

"Oh, come on, Squire—there's room enough in the churchyard. There's room for a hundred."

"They're slicing the ears for the rings," one of the Cutler twins screeched.

"Isaac," Hunt yelled, "did you send someone for Pastor Dorset or not? Did I instruct you to or did I not?"

He backed out of that. Let Pastor Dorset settle it. People were coming across the meadows from the direction of Buskin's farm. The roar of guns must have been heard for miles around, and there were children running ahead of the women.

"Keep them all away," Hunt growled. "Don't any of you have any sense? Keep the children away. Keep the women away. As a matter of fact, I don't want anyone but Pastor Dorset here. Naham! Where the devil is Naham Buskin?"

"Here! Here!" Buskin shouted. He was at the wall, staring at the carnage.

"Can you give us a wagon to put the bodies in?"

"That curses the wagon."

"Don't be such a superstitious fool," Saxon, the under-taker, told him. "If you don't give us a wagon, you'll have those poor souls swelling up like sausage in the sun and stinking too."

Buskin took off toward his house, and Hunt turned to me and asked:

"What does the paper say?"

"Why?"

"Because the money and the gold's going to be re-turned—every bit of it."

"To whom?"

"To the British. Who else?"

"How?"

"Now isn't that a fine question to ask me, when I'm just about going out of my mind with what to do next?"

"Very well," I said. "It's a letter to his wife. He never finished it. It's an intimate kind of thing, and he talks about his love for her and his love for his children, three children I believe—"

"Feversham, that's out of the whole cloth."

"Go to hell!" I told him, and threw the letter in his face and stalked away.

An hour later, I rode through my front gate and gave my horse to Rodney Stephan, who immediately began to question me about the battle. I shook my head and went into the surgery to get out of my bloody boots and clothes and clean myself, and while I was undressing, Alice came in. She gasped with horror at the pile of bloodstained garments.

"What happened?" she whispered. "I heard the guns."

I stood there naked, looking down at my skinny shanks, at the great purple gash in my left thigh.

"Please bring me my robe," I said to her.

I washed at my surgery sink, and then she came with the robe and I wrapped it around me and sat down on a stool, hunched over and shivering.

"Are you sick?"

I shook my head.

She brought me a cup of hot broth, and I drank it and felt somewhat better. She took the clothes and my boots away.

"Get dressed, Evan," she said gently. "There is some meat and bread to the table, and you must eat."

I smiled for the first time in this day that had begun so very early and had already lasted an eternity into what was only early afternoon. I went up to my room and dressed, and while I was there I heard the sounds of men and horses at the front gate, and then when I came down, they rode off. Alice was waiting in the dining room, but I stepped out of the house to call to Rodney Stephan and ask him what the commotion was.

"The men on the hunt. They would I went with them, and I told them no, I cannot."

"What hunt?"

"They hunt the Hessian boy. They rouse up the whole neighborhood. There never was such a hunt, Doctor Feversham."

"Then they haven't caught him yet?"

"No, sir."

I sat at the table without appetite but drank coffee greedily, and Alice watched me and waited, and finally said, "It will be better if you talk about it, Evan. You will set it better in your heart and mind and not be in such a turmoil."

"How do you know what turmoil I am in?"

"Who could not know? Why don't you tell me?"

Then I told her. I told her all that had happened since I went into the Center and the tavern in the morning, and of the killing at Buskin's farm and all the rest of it. She took it well and wept no useless tears, but sat there regarding me thoughtfully and with affection.

"What shall I say, Evan?"

I shook my head vainly.

"No words mean anything, do they? Do you remember when Mrs. Cartwright's little girl died, and you thought you could save her, and then—"

I nodded. I remembered it well indeed.

"Strange," Alice said, "because when I first knew you, I thought that you and Abe Hunt would be such good friends; there is so much in both of you that is alike."

"Then you know me very little," I answered with annoyance.

"No, Evan. Don't be provoked with me. You hate the Squire so, you no longer see him as a man or a human being."

"More than he hates me?"

"I don't know who hates the other more, only that hate begets hate, and where does it end? What do we say when we go to the church on Sunday? God forgive us? And what can that possibly mean?"

"Since I don't go to your church," I reminded her, "that is not my problem." I was trying to strike back at her. "Still I suspect that Dorset will take a text to the effect that he who lives by the sword will die by the sword, and that covers all contingencies, doesn't it?"

"You know you don't believe any of that."

"I don't know what I believe anymore. I can only tell you that at this moment I am peculiarly without belief or faith or grace or any others of those words we use so glibly as an argument that men are in some way different from animals."

"Evan, aren't you forgetting how afraid they were?"

"Who?"

"Our people."

"Your people."

"My people then," she said. "And don't you think Squire Hunt was afraid? And suppose it had been the other way and the Hessians had left you and the rest of the militia lying in your blood—?"

"What the devil are you trying to say?"

"I am only trying to say that Abe Hunt is not just a murderer. Or else all war is murder and I no longer know what is right and wrong; but I know Abe Hunt. He courted me before I married Alex, and then when Alex died, I leaned on him and he was like a rock." And seeing the look on my face she added, "No, he's not jealous, and he's married with five children, but I only want you to understand that he isn't entirely the person you think he is. He's honest and loyal, and his reputation is for the best magistrate in western Connecticut, and if he says the money and the jewels will go back to the British, somehow they will—"

I shook my head, trying to follow what she was saying and go with her point. "He will return the money. He's a righteous man. You Puritans are an amazing lot, and most amazing is your corner on righteousness."

"And now you're angry."

"Not at all! Oh, no. Myself angry? No indeed." And being entirely without any grounds for my rage, I slammed my chair back and stamped out of the room, leaving her sitting there and looking after me with that strange expression of inscrutable patience that only a woman can wear.

I had three sick people that afternoon: Stickham, the cobbler, who had spring rash; Mrs. Elliott with the assorted agonies attending her change of life; and Mrs. Curtis with a bad cut in her son's foot. All three of them wanted only to chatter about the battle and the Hessian who had escaped, and there was much talk of bolting doors and shuttering windows until I declared that I wanted no more sound out of any of them. Otherwise, I could look out of our front door, for we are highly and beautifully situated, and see the whole country thereabout, and see for myself that the chase and hunt after the Hessian had become a local preoccupation. Men on horseback were coursing across meadows and plowed fields as if they had never driven off the old Tory foxhunters at gunpoint, and there was hooting and shouting and the firing of guns in the distance.

Serving at dinner, Rodney Stephan told us that they had trapped the Hessian at the Squeehunk Rockface and that somehow he had managed to claw his way up its hundred and fifty feet of ragged cliff and over the top. They lost him there, and then, later that night, we heard hounds baying in the distance. It had turned cold with sundown, and I was sitting in front of the fire with Alice, trying to concentrate on the latest edition of the *Advertiser,* when we began to hear the hounds calling.

Alice, working over petitpoint, looked up finally and asked me how old I thought the Hessian drummer boy might be.

"Fifteen, sixteen perhaps. The German regiments enlist them at the age of twelve."

"How dreadful!"

"Indeed? I saw a drummer boy of twelve die at Monmouth—our own—and the Cutler twins are what, thirteen? Fourteen?"

"What have they to do with it?"

"They were at the ambush."

"Oh." Then she went back to her petitpoint, and again, from far off, we heard the baying of the hounds. Usually, it's a sound I love and one that takes me back to the few good days of my youth, but tonight it was intolerable.

"What will they do if they catch him?" Alice asked me.

"Alive?"

"Today is your day to be grotesque."

"Try him."

"For what? For running away? For being a Hessian?"

"For the murder of Saul Clamberham."

"You're being vile tonight. I trust you know how perfectly vile you are being."

"It's a vile night."

"Don't you understand that people are afraid of him?"

I went back to the *Advertiser* and permitted myself silent opinions on the men who edit papers in the colonies, and she went back to the petitpoint, but not for long.

"Can't we know what happened to him?"

"Call Rodney Stephan and ask him."

"How will he know?"

"If there's anything to know, he'll know it."

She stared at me for a long moment, and then, putting aside her work, she went to the door and called out for Rodney Stephan. The baying of the hounds was almost inaudible in the distance.

He came to the door with a silver tray that he was polishing. I had eleven pieces of good silver that were all that remained of my father's estate, and he polished them constantly, for he was one of those men who could never sit for even a moment with idle hands but must work always at this or that.

"Have they caught the Hessian boy?" she asked him.

"No, ma'am."

"How do you know?"

"Well, for one thing, Goody Feversham, there's the baying of the hounds. They wouldn't sing if they weren't on scent."

"Come on now," I said, "you know a hunting hound —and he'll leave any scent if he comes on bear or deer. They had nothing to prime him with."

"Begging you, Doctor, they had the drum. The lad threw it away."

I remembered that now, but it wasn't enough. You couldn't track a man with the bastard dogs they raised on the Ridge.

Rodney Stephan nodded. "Still, they ain't found him. Oscar would hear at the inn, and he said he'd send his boy with the news. I promised him a bag of Swedes. They're not at their best after the long winter," he explained apologetically. "I knew you'd want the news."

"Do you think they'll take him?" Alice asked.

"Sooner or later, Goody Feversham. Where's he to go? I hold no malice, for a lad's a lad, but where's he to go?"

"It took strength and determination to go over that rock face."

"Aye, he's nimble, be sure, and if he has any nose for the land, he'll go into the big swamp. That's the direction of the song—listen to them!"

Very faint and far off, we heard the hounds—and then no sound at all. We looked at each other.

"I'll tell ye if the Latham lad shows."

But we went to bed and slept, and morning came, and there was no sign of Oscar Latham's boy to tell us that the Hessian had been taken and to collect his prize of Swedes. As the day wore on, my patients reflected one aspect or another of what had happened, and not one of them but dwelt on what a great and glorious victory it was. Bosley Crippit, the clerk and recorder, who chronically suffered from half a century of vainly attempting to drink himself to death and as a result passed his water with agony, kept boring me through his pain with a comparative analysis of every battle fought during the years of the war; and he declared, his glee punctured only by whimpers of agony, that proportionately speaking, what they already called "The Battle of Buskin Farm" was the greatest victory of all.

"For mind you, Doctor Feversham, there is no casualty on our side, not one single blessed scratch, while the wrath of the Lord smote the Hessians, root and branch. Totality cannot be exceeded."

"What?" I demanded.

"I said totality cannot be exceeded."

"That's what I thought you said."

"Benjamin Franklin."

"What do you mean, Benjamin Franklin? Did he say that?"

"Something of the sort. He's a prominent man in Philadelphia, old but very active. Very active."

"I have heard of him."

"I thought possibly not, you being an Englishman."

"I have been here in this land eleven years, Mr.

Crippit, and during that time I have heard of Mr. Franklin on various occasions. I think no rum for a fortnight. No beer. No wine."

It would make no difference with the poor devil; it was only my own petty revenge.

After my morning surgery, Rodney Stephan came in and told me that the Hessian was still untaken, and that Raymond Heather's boy, Jacob, desired to speak with me.

"Is he ill?"

"The Hessian?"

"Oh, no, the Heather lad."

"He seems spry."

"And where did they lose the Hessian?"

"In the great swamp," Rodney Stephan answered, "and so long as he's in there they'll not take him, but he'll die there. He'll perish there surely."

"I'll see the boy," I said.

Rodney Stephan brought Jacob Heather into the surgery, and the small, freckled, orange-haired lad stood there waiting and licking his lips until I told Rodney Stephan to go and leave us private.

"Which is what you desire," I said to the boy.

"Yes, sir. My father said I was not to beseech thee if another stood by."

"Well, we're alone, Jacob."

"Yes, sir. My father says, thee must come and the need is very great, sir, Doctor Feversham."

"Who is sick? Not your mother?"

He shook his head.

"The baby?"

"I cannot tell thee."

"Or you will not! Come now, Jacob," I declared with annoyance. "It's four long miles to your place, and you

want me to ride over there without knowing how or
why?"

"Yes, sir."

I stared at him a long moment, and then suddenly I
understood, and said gently, "All right, lad. You wait
outside." Then I told Rodney Stephan to harness the
chaise and I told my wife that I was off to Heather's,
where there was illness.

5

The Refuge

Sitting next to me in the buggy, the boy asked me, "Doctor Feversham, did thee kill any Hessians?"

"No."

"Why?"

He was filled with something sour, a kind of small boy agony that I could only sense, and I answered his question in the most direct way I could. "I had no gun," I told him.

He considered that for a minute or so, and then said, "Would thee have killed a Hessian if thee had a gun?"

It was my turn to consider. "I don't know," I answered finally. "I am a physician. That makes a difference. You see, if I had a gun, then the act would be having the gun. Do you understand me?"

The boy shook his head and was silent for a time. "I should not have brought the news," he said at last.

"Did your father say that?"

"No."

"You did what you had to do."

"How does a man know what he has to do?" he asked, a note of woe in his voice.

"You are a boy, not a man."

"My father says he will not speak me as a boy, he speaks me as a man."

"How old are you, Jacob?"

"Twelve years."

I have no children, and what was I to say to him? We drove on in silence to the Heather place, and there Raymond was standing in front of his house, awaiting me. Heather is a man of middling height, pale blue eyes and a long, gentle face. His strength was not apparent, for his lack of animosity was so consistent that one tended to take it for weakness. He greeted me warmly, trying to find a way into explanations, but I said shortly:

"Take this bottle of rum and tell them inside that I want hot water—boiling, do you understand, boiling."

We were on our way to the house.

"Water the horse," I told Jacob.

"Then Jacob—" Raymond began.

"No, Jacob said nothing, and neither am I foolish, Raymond. Is it a bullet?"

"Yes."

"Where?"

"In the back, over the shoulder blade."

Sarah opened the door for us, her lovely round face clouded and troubled.

"I want boiling water and clean linen," I snapped at her, "and I want it as quickly as possible. Where is he?"

Raymond led the way upstairs and into the small room under the eaves where Jacob slept. I had never been upstairs in their house before, but it was no different from the other farmhouses on the Ridge, the rooms too small, the ceiling too low, chilled in winter and hot boxes in summer. The bed was low and narrow, as they make their children's beds, and the Hessian lay there, his eyes closed, moaning slightly, while Sally, Raymond's sixteen-year-old daughter, wiped his brow with a damp cloth. They had put a quilt over the Hessian. His long, damp and dirty flaxen hair was spread across the pillow, and the freckles stood out sharply on his ash-colored skin.

He could not have been much older than Sally, the yellow down on his cheeks still unshaven, and his scratched, bruised hands were long-fingered and rather delicate. The Heathers had taken off his boots and his jacket and his breeches, leaving him in his singlet.

I felt his forehead, which was all aflame with the kind of heat that bodes no good and little hope, and then I told Sally to bring me soap and water for my hands. There are doctors who believe otherwise, but to me dirt is evil, in a wound or on a doctor's hands.

"Help me turn him on his belly," I said to Raymond.

Between us, we turned him over, the boy being heavier than I might have imagined. Raymond had put a pad on the hole in his back and a bandage to hold it there, which at least stopped the bleeding, and now I cut it away, revealing a hole the size of a farthing. The blood was thick there, half clotted.

"Was the blood flowing when you found him?"

"Slow," Raymond replied.

"Then you don't know what he lost in the way of blood?"

Raymond shook his head. "But enough. Look at his skin."

"That's a spent rifle ball, thank God, and no wound he suffered over by Buskin's. I was afraid I'd find a hole in his back the size of my fist, and the life gone out of him. They've been taking potshots at him all of yesterday and no sight of him this morning, so he must have taken the ball before the sun went down and lived with it the night through, and now he's got a wretched fever from the wound. Come on, Sally, where's the soap and water!"

She brought in the basin of warm water, and I washed my hands, telling her to bring candles, the light in the room was so poor; and then I told her to remain there, meeting Raymond's eye. "It's quite all right—she's old enough to see this." I was probing gently for the bullet, and the Hessian boy suddenly came into consciousness and screamed with pain. "Hold him," I snapped at Raymond. "Damn it, do you want me to kill him with the probe? Hold him. Put your knee in his back and get on the bed. Hold him down. I don't want him moving. Sally, get that damn candle over here!"

"The wax is dripping."

"Let it drip."

Sarah entered the room and handed Sally a second candle, and now I touched the bullet, felt the touch, and was brought back not only in my mind but with a memory of my entire being to the hundred times I had done this on some blood-stinking battlefield, probing into the flesh of some poor boy—and they were always boys— to find a bullet, or a piece of iron or a rusty nail out of grapeshot, and the screaming under the pain as I drove my probe here and there, touching nerves, touching the fiber of life and evoking the ultimate indignity.

I took the forceps and went in, trying to hold the flesh apart with the probe, but the hole was too small, and I had to open the wound with a scalpel. When I did, the yellow pus poured out. I glanced at Sally and said sharply:

"Look smart, girl, and learn something, and mind what you're doing!"

I know the sign of sickness, and the last thing I wanted was for her to throw up over the wound. Sarah handed me pieces of clean linen, and the boy's screaming became a whimper as I found the bullet and drew it forth. The wound was bleeding freely now, and Sarah, one of those women who is never rattled and never loses her head, handed me piece after piece of the linen to wipe away the blood and the pus.

"He'll bleed to death," Sally whispered.

"No he won't, my girl, and you've been a good one and just stick to it. That's the evil humor bleeding out, and God willing it takes the pus with it. If it festers inside, believe me, he won't live to see tomorrow, so you just grit your teeth and keep the light with me and tell yourself I've taken more bullets out of men than you've cracked walnuts."

I cleaned the wound thoroughly, and while I was thus engaged, the boy's struggling stopped, and Sally cried out, "He's dead!"

"No more than you are. Now look you, Sally," I said, as I took up my needle and gut, "I am going to sew the wound and you keep the light on me, and just remember that I'm sewing in his life, and you'll learn a little craft that may do you well someday."

With that, I took five stitches in the wound, and then made a pad for it. The boy had fainted, which made it somewhat easier to bandage across his chest and back, and then we laid him out on the bed and made him easy. His breath was slow but even now, and when I took his pulse, it was at one hundred and ten, which was only to be expected after the shock of the operation. I thought his fever to be a trifle less, but one never knows surely. I covered him over with the quilt and told them that someone would have to stay with him and watch him and put cold compresses to his brow. The hot water that I had dipped my instruments in had cooled, so I cleaned them out of a fresh kettle Sarah brought me, and then washed my hands and packed my bag.

"Pull a chair by his bed," I said to Sally, "for this is your thing now, and it's a thing of the spirit, Sally. There is no more I can do. The next day or so will tell whether he lives or dies, and all we can do for the fever is to cool his brow and cool his wrists, and that's your task. Your father and mother have other chores."

"Thank thee. I will do what I may," she answered seriously.

Then we left them and went down the stairs to the kitchen, where Sarah put coffee and bread and butter and cheese on the table, and I was able to sit for a moment and stretch my legs. When I lifted the cup of coffee, I saw that my hand was trembling and realized that the Hessian boy meant far more to me than the simple act of removing a bullet from a wounded man. Jacob and Annie, his four-year-old sister, were there in the kitchen, silent and wide-eyed with fright at the screams they had heard, but the baby, Joanna, had slept peacefully through it all. Raymond joined me at the table and ate hungrily.

"I served no dinner today," Sarah said apologetically. "Thee must know, Doctor Feversham, that we are not with ourselves today. Thee understand."

I didn't know whether I understood or not. Something

had been absent in that house, for which absence she apologized, but I was by no means sure that I understood what was absent—nor indeed that I understood very much about Quakers at all. On and off through the years, I had known or been in relationship with Quakers and some Quaker families as well, not all of them like the Heathers, but with enough similarity among them for me to have a sense of them; yet as often as I felt I had it, it eluded me. And in my mind now, in response to Sarah Heather's curious statement, there was evoked only the memory of the sad little Catholic priest, afflicted with boils and riding his donkey through this cold and strange Protestant land.

"Please eat and comfort thee, Doctor Feversham," she said.

Her bread was good and so was her country cheese and fresh-churned sweet butter, and like Raymond, I had been the day without food. I ate and considered the irresponsibility of fate, that it should place me and Raymond and the lad Jacob here, with the Hessian drummer boy upstairs, and I began to think of consequences, when Raymond asked me:

"Will he live, Doctor?"

"As God wills—and if God wills him to live, then so much the greater pleasure for Abraham Hunt when he hangs him."

"Ah, no!" Sarah exclaimed. "Squire Hunt is a just man!"

"Sarah, we are all just men, and we make the rules of justice. Hunt will hold a court-martial, and I have no doubt that General Packenham will come over from New Haven to preside, and what will they find? That he participated in the hanging of Saul Clamberham. So they will do justice—unless they shoot him down on sight."

Sarah shook her head. "Ah, no—no, no, Doctor. I know what thee must feel to be a Catholic here in our land and all the little hurts that come to thee, but thee judge us too sharply."

"Not you, Sarah. I judge others."

"No, don't—please, dear friend. We will pray and we will be heard."

"I am afraid, Sarah, that the doctor is right."

"We will pray," she said calmly.

"No, Sarah—thee don't understand me. We will pray, but the doctor is right. They will take the boy and hang him."

"No!"

"Believe me, Sarah," I said. "They will."

"Then," she said calmly, "they shall not take the boy."

"Oh?" And I looked at Raymond.

Then there was silence, and the silence went on and on, and finally Raymond said softly, "We live here by sufferance. I am not pleading anything, Doctor Feversham. I am only a cobbler and a farmer, and thee is a man of great education and experience, and I am honored by thy friendship. But thee understand as I do what it is to live in a place by sufferance. What shall I do?"

"I can't tell you that, Raymond."

"What will thee do?"

"It is not mine to do anything. I am a physician. I never asked the nationality of a stricken man. I have treated Englishman and American and made no preference."

"Will thee turn the lad over to Squire Hunt?"

"You ask me that, Raymond?"

"Yet thee live by sufferance even as I do."

"The boy is under your roof, Raymond, not mine. My way is an easy way. I close my bag and I drive away. How can I tell you what your way should be?"

"He doesn't ask what his way should be," Sarah said with some asperity. "He knows his way, as I know my way. He asks what thee will do."

"I will go home to my house and my surgery and do my business, Sarah, which is something I think you should know."

Sarah came around the table now, and pulled out the chair facing me, and sat down. She studied me for a long moment, her lovely gray eyes evenly fixed upon mine, her honey-colored hair loosened somewhat in all the excitement and lying upon her neck like a collar, reminding me again of that sick feeling of hopelessness and desire I felt almost every time I laid eyes upon her.

"Now let me say this to thee, Evan Feversham. There is no Hessian. The Hessian is gone forever, and so I will swear and perjure myself before God. Up in bed lies my nephew from Pennsylvania, who grew up in the Dutch country there, where there are plenty of our people, and so it will be said, and Raymond will bury his uniform and all signs of war forever. We will be very quiet here, and in six months it will all be forgotten."

"Sarah, Sarah," Raymond sighed.

"Who knows," I said. "Perhaps—"

"We don't live alone. If now was wintertime, it might be, but in May—"

"We will do what we must, and God will provide," Sarah said calmly.

"Yes, we will do what we must," Raymond agreed.

At home at supper that night, I said nothing and offered no explanations to Alice, for there were other ears to hear; but once we sat by the fire, I told my wife what had transpired.

"But he's a Hessian!" was her first reaction.

"Alice, Alice—he's a boy."

"And you're so sure that Abe Hunt will hang a boy."

"No, I am not sure, but I can make a good guess as to what he will do. He will hold a court-martial—and then the thing will run wild. No, I am not going to guess. I know only one thing, that the Heathers are two of the few Christians I have ever met in this Christian land, and I will not betray Sarah Heather and I will not question any decision she makes."

"And you will also think whatever Sarah Heather desires you to think."

"Sarah Heather is happily married, and I like to think that I am too."

"And I suppose you will tell me someday that you will not question any decision I make—oh, yes, you will indeed."

"I meant nothing of the kind."

"Of what kind?"

"Alice, Alice, if the boy were here now, wouldn't I abide by what you willed?"

"If I said turn him over to Abraham Hunt?"

Without replying, I got up and began to poke about the room.

"Well, sir, Doctor Feversham?"

"Where is my pipe?"

"Why don't you say the truth for once?"

"No," I answered. "I would not abide by your decision if you said turn him over to Abe Hunt." I found my pipe, stuffed it full of tobacco, and went to the fireplace for an ember. "Because war is a word to you," I said.

"Because you have never seen deserters hanged and even whipped to death."

"In your army, not in ours," she said bitterly.

"Your army! My army! Christ Almighty, was this leg of mine torn in shreds in my army? Am I suddenly a loyal Englishman every time you lose your temper with me?"

"Oh, Evan—don't let us build this any more. I am sorry."

"And what of the boy?"

"You think I'd turn him in?" she cried. "Is that what you think of me?"

"I never thought that of you. Would I have taken you into my confidence if I had thought that of you? Only—"

"We'll say no more about it."

"No more," I agreed.

"Only it makes no sense. How can they hide him?"

"I don't know."

Yet the following afternoon, when I came to the Heather place, it was less a question of sheltering him than of having a live Hessian to shelter. "Sally is with him," Sarah said to me. "Evan, I'm afraid for the lad." She poured water for me, and while I washed she told me how Sally had scarcely left his side through all the night.

The weather had changed, and all afternoon it had rained steadily. As I went up the stairs, the rain beat its tattoo all over the little house. Jacob and his small sister, Annie, watched me from the shelter of their parents' room, their heads out to see what horrors I brought with me this time, and in the tiny room where the Hessian lay, Sally greeted me with a face of woe and weariness. Somehow, this twenty-four hours had taken the flush of childhood out of her face and turned her into a woman, and I noticed how like her mother she appeared.

"Evan," she pleaded, calling me by my Christian name, as her mother did, "Evan, don't let him die. He's kind and good—Evan, please, please—"

The boy was watching us now, his eyes open, his eyes moving from Sally to me. Sally had somehow cleaned his hair and his face, and now his hair lay like silk on the pillow, and with the almost translucent pallor of his skin, he appeared strangely childlike.

"Who said he's going to die? No more nonsense. Boy," I said to him, "can you turn over?" And then I asked Sally, "Does he know English?"

"He knows English, but he's out of his head. He doesn't know what thee is saying."

"Then help me turn him over."

The boy resisted, but his strength was small and we turned him on his stomach. "Can you hold him?" I asked Sally. "Or will you bring your father?"

"I can hold him. Perhaps he'll know me." And then she said to the boy, "Hans—Hans, listen. We help thee. Believe me. Have faith in me."

"How do you know his name is Hans?" I asked her as I cut away the bandage. "How do you know he's so kind and good?"

"Because we spoke this morning."

I took the bandage off. The wound was swollen with pus, the pus oozing out from between the sutures. When I touched the area, the boy groaned with pain. I cut the sutures, opened the wound and let it drain.

"Did you give him to eat?" I asked Sally.

"A little broth. A cup."

"Did he hold it down?"

"Yes. And he drank water, a lot of water."

"That's good, good."

"Will he die?"

"I don't know, Sally."

The draining of the wound had eased him, and he appeared to be sleeping now.

"Now, look you, girl, he's easy now, and I am going to leave the wound open and let it drain. I'll stay here by his side, and you go downstairs and eat some food, then have a nap."

"He needs me."

"He does not need you now, Sally. If he needs anyone, he needs me, and I shall do whatever can be done. So get out of here and don't put your face through that door until I call you."

"Because he's dying?" she asked woefully.

"Because he is not dying. Now go!"

Then I sat there alone in the tiny room, while outside the daylight began to fade. Perhaps a half hour passed, the Hessian groaning now and then but not moving, which pleased me for his wound was still and open. Sarah came with two lit candles, and asked me would I eat something.

"No, dear lady, but send Jacob to my wife, and let him tell her that I will be here possibly through the night. Caution him to tell her alone and not in front of my man, Rodney Stephan. Is Sally asleep?"

"Yes. Evan, what is this Hessian boy in her life?"

"She's your daughter, not mine."

"Will he live, Evan?"

"I don't know. When a wound decays into ill humor and the pus builds up and a fever mounts—then it is his life in his own hands, and if the life force inside of him is strong enough, he will overcome the pus and break the fever. Otherwise, he will die. I've seen this so many times, always the same. Now touch him—touch his brow."

"He's burning," she said.

"Yes. If it breaks before morning, he will live." I shrugged. "That's all."

"Poor Sally, poor child, she has taken his life upon herself."

"What do you mean by that?" I asked her.

"I am not sure that I know or that I can explain it. Tell me, Evan, in thy faith is there grace?"

"If you are fortunate. I am not fortunate. What about Sally?"

"Did thee know that they buried the Hessians in the Congregational churchyard?"

"That was generous of them."

"Thee hate too much, Evan."

"Perhaps. I find very little to love in this world. Look now, I am going to close up the wound, and then I will have to raise him up to bandage him. Will you send Raymond up here to help me?"

She nodded and left, and a few minutes later, Raymond Heather appeared. I closed the wound and put a pad upon it, and then we turned the lad and Raymond held him up while I made a bandage around his chest and back. He came awake into a kind of semiconsciousness, and looked at us and smiled gently, as a child does.

"I have two shillings for payment," Raymond said, "and I am afraid thee must take the rest in kind."

"Raymond, Raymond—"

We stared at each other a long moment, and then he nodded and said, "I am sorry. I won't speak of it again." He stood awkwardly. "We go to bed soon. Shall I stay with thee?"

I shook my head.

"Will thee call me if thee need me?"

"I'll call you, Raymond."

"I sleep lightly. Tap on the door of our room."

"If I need you, Raymond."

Then he left, and I sat alone with the Hessian, as I have sat with a man or a woman or a child, sick or dying or finding life, so many times that I cannot remember. I don't know what I bring to them, if indeed anything at all; but perhaps I take something from them. It was the only religion I had remaining to me. No one, not my wife, not any soul, not even the priest to whom I had made a sort of confession a few days before, knew what a desolate wasteland my life was or what a nightmare my thoughts became when I saw myself as a meaningless fragment on this rocky ridge of land in a place called Connecticut, with no one with whom I could exchange a word or an idea that was meaningful to me. So perhaps I gave something of value to the sick or the dying, or perhaps I took something from them; whatever the case, I found some peace there, a kind of quietude where my thoughts calmed and where some sort of prayer for forgiveness and healing worked itself out in my soul.

It became night, and in the stillness the voices of the night asserted themselves, and besides the hoarse breathing of the Hessian boy, I could hear the footsteps of creatures outside, the shrill cry of an owl, the scraping of the raccoons as they came to investigate the place of people, the angry bark of the dogs and in the distance the wild cry of the loons in the great swamp.

The Hessian groaned. I felt his brow, and the fever burned like fire. It was close to the time when he would either live or die, but not go on with the fire inside of his veins.

And then the door opened, and Sally came into the room. The candles had burned low, and she brought new ones to refurbish the light; and after they were lit, she sat down across the bed from me, explaining quietly:

"I know he will live or die now, so it is better that I be here, is it not?"

"Perhaps," I said.

"He will only live if his spirit quickens," she said simply.

"And you will quicken it, Sally?" I asked, not sardonically but with actual curiosity.

"Yes."

"Tell me how."

"With love," she said. "I love him."

"Child, you don't even know him."

"I know him well, Evan Feversham," she replied with great dignity. "We spoke yesterday. And I found him, so his life is in my hand, is it not?"

"How do you mean, you found him?"

"Did not my father tell thee?"

"No. We didn't speak of how he came to you. I meant to ask him but I never did."

"He was in the swamp, and he came out of there and through the woods and across our meadow, and he hid himself in the haypile in the barn. When I came in the morning to feed the chickens, I saw his hand from under the hay. I wasn't afraid. Then I took the hay away and wakened him, and there was no fear between us. And then I went for my father, who carried him into the house."

"But why do you say you love him?" I insisted. "Unless you speak of your faith, which I suppose is to love every person if you can."

"That is one way," she said calmly, as if she were talking about the weather, about the rain that afternoon and about the bright moon that now shone in the sky. "I love him another way. I love him as a woman loves a man."

"Aren't you being foolish?" I asked, provoked and irritated by her calm and certainty. "He's not a man. He's a boy, and you're only a child. How can you love him? You don't know him. He's a stranger."

"There are no strangers to us."

"Have you spoken of this to your mother or father?"

"No, only to thee, to explain why I must stay here. Thee will let me stay here."

"If you wish. But I must say I think you are talking romantic nonsense, and if you were my own daughter, I would shake some sense into your foolish head."

"Then I must be grateful I am not thy daughter, Doctor Feversham, as much as I admire thee."

"I thank you for your admiration, Sally Heather, and if you wish me to consider you a woman rather than a child, you may begin by trying to act like a woman and not like a silly little girl."

Her eyes moistened and filled with tears.

"We'll say no more about it," I said. "I am a physician and used to confidences, so don't feel that yours are misplaced. Now if you can sit quietly, you may remain, and if you want work to do, see that the cloth on his brow is kept wet and cold."

Time passed, and we sat in silence, and then finally I took out my watch and looked at it. It was half past four in the morning, and the boy was breathing easier now. I took the cloth off his forehead and laid my hand against it. He was cool.

"That's it," I whispered to Sally. "The fever has broken. He's asleep now. It's real sleep." I stood up. "You can leave him."

She shook her head.

"As you wish."

I went downstairs, and there was hot water in a kettle in the embers in the fireplace. I made myself a cup of coffee, mixing the cold leftovers of the night before with the hot water in the kettle. At best war coffee bore only a thin resemblance to the real thing, and this was far from the best; but it warmed my stomach and the way I felt, I cared little about the taste of coffee. I was full of that good thing a doctor has when someone he is treating draws back from the doors of death, and this together with a lack of sleep and food gave me a delightful sense of euphoria.

Then I went to the door and stepped out into the cool, rain-washed morning air, remaining there for a moment or two, breathing deeply, and staring with pleasure at the east where pink and rose color flamed in advance of the sun. Raymond came from the cowbarn, carrying two pails of frothy milk, and he set them down carefully in his coldpit and then joined me at the door.

"The boy will live," I said, in answer to his unspoken question.

"Thank God."

I studied him curiously, wondering what link connected all of these folk to an unbidden stranger; and I must confess that I envied him too, not only for his wife—which was one kind of envy—but for the simple certainty of his actions.

"Yes, and that solves nothing. This boy—"

"His name is Hans Pohl," Raymond said. "He is sixteen years and nine months of age, and he has been in America three years already. His father was a sergeant and he was born into the camp, but that is not to say he is a lost soul—"

"Raymond," I interrupted, "how the devil do you know not only his name but his character as well?"

"All this Sally told me. He spoke to her yesterday."

"And Sally is the judge of his character?"

Raymond smiled and shook his head, as if any explanation would be beyond me—as perhaps it might have been.

6

Hans Pohl

IN THE ORDINARY COURSE of things, Abraham Hunt was not a patient of mine. He preferred to take his infrequent ailments to Toby Benson, the town barber, who carried enough soil under his fingernails to plant a garden, who took snuff in excess, used a kerchief three and four weeks without washing, and knew two things about what he called "medicine"—namely leeching and bleeding. I admit to bitterness, but this local monstrosity had bled half a dozen citizens into an early grave and had impeded the normal healing process in at least a hundred others. And since Squire Hunt was by no means unintelligent, when he contracted gout, he brought it to me.

A few hours after I had returned home from Raymond Heather's place to a cold breakfast and the increasing petulance of my wife, Hunt brought his swollen foot into my surgery. It took the help of Rodney Stephan to get his boot off, and when I asked him why on earth he didn't ride in a slipper, he looked at me with such cold disdain that I pursued his vanity no further.

"Gout?" he asked me.

I prodded it a bit more than necessary, and then agreed with his diagnosis.

"What can you do for me?" he demanded.

"Did you catch the Hessian?" I couldn't help asking him.

"Oh? We shall—we shall indeed, Feversham."

"Who knows? He could be off the Ridge and back down to Saugatuck, couldn't he? Time enough by now."

"With a bullet in his back?"

"What?"

"A bullet, Feversham. Hey you there, Rodney Stephan," he shouted at the easily befuddled halfbreed Indian who was my gardener and man about the house, "why have you not told your master about the bullet in the Hessian's back?"

Rodney Stephan shook his head. He knew me well enough to know that I would want the Hessian to get clear; then why tell me of new misery?

"So he's dead," I said to Hunt.

"Oh, no. I did not say that. I said he caught a bullet, and we found a nice, likely sum of blood. He went into the great swamp, and he'll come out, or there he'll die. I can wait. I have time. No Hessian will leave this ridge alive—not while I'm here, Feversham."

I prodded his gout again, and he winced and demanded to know what I thought I was about.

"About this foot of yours. It's a wretched mess."

"It's gout, as you say. You're a physician, Feversham. Do something about it."

"Oh, no. That's up to you."

"What?"

"I'll tell you what, Squire. You go on eating the way

you have been eating, meat three times a day, beefsteak as raw as when it lived, and filling your belly full of port wine and rum and beer—well, you'll have two gouty legs, not one," I finished with some satisfaction.

"I am what I am, Feversham."

"You are what you eat, more likely—which is gout. So that's it, Squire. A fortnight without meat or drink; gruel and bread twice a day and clean water, and you'll have a normal foot again."

"Gruel twice a day?"

"Gruel twice a day—precisely."

It was poor revenge, and I felt thwarted and quite disgusted with myself, and suddenly I looked up at Hunt, and he was smiling at me.

"You have me, Feversham."

"There's no other cure for it. I'm sorry."

"By God, I believe you are sorry," he said.

That day, I did not go over to Heather's place. For one thing, I was kept in my surgery with the six Clementine children, all of them wormy and snotty and quincy, and three of them with festering splinters. They were Danbury people, and had taken half a day to come to me and were as poor as churchmice, but I could not turn them away.

At dinner, Alice was quiet, turned in on her own thoughts and lost in melancholy. She had bought a rooster and seven hens, that we might begin to have our own eggs, but she fended all my questions about poultry. First I felt that she had taken added umbrage at my staying the night at Raymond's place; but when I attempted to explain that the very thought of anything between myself and Sarah Heather was of the stuff of fevered imagination, she snapped at me:

"Don't be a fool, Evan, or take me for one. You've been in love with that woman since the first day you laid eyes upon her."

"You have told me repeatedly," I pointed out, "that I am not capable of loving anyone."

"No." She shook her head. "Let's not go that way."

"Although, the fact is—"

"Oh, stop it," she said. "Believe me, I am not troubled by any thoughts of yours concerning Sarah Heather, and I know quite well that there is nothing there. Underneath that saintly face of hers a very dull woman resides, and I only wish you could spend a week with her and be properly bored."

"Then what are you so morose over?"

She didn't answer immediately, but a little while later she came to it and admitted that she had talked with Abraham Hunt.

"About what?"

"The Hessian."

"You didn't—"

"Really, Evan. You can be a pig about things."

"I am sorry."

Silence again, and then she said, "No, I did not tell him where the Hessian is. I only asked him what he would do with him if they took him."

"To which he said?"

"They would try him and hang him."

"How splendid! They will not try him and attempt to discover just what he is guilty of. No, indeed. They will try him and hang. First the verdict, then the trial."

"Evan," she said, her voice suddenly different, "try to understand. You are a European, and I have never quite comprehended what our little villages here on this continent mean to you, or how you look upon the people

we are. But through all the long years of this war,
eighteen boys have gone out of our little township and
have never returned. I don't think they ever will. Do
you wonder that we feel a certain bitterness toward our
enemies, toward men who fight and kill for hire?"

"Bitterness or plain hatred?"

"Both, I suppose. Is it so strange?"

"Perhaps not. I don't know. I can't judge."

"Do you imagine that I enjoy the thought that they
might hang this man?"

"He's only a boy, not a man."

"And boys fight the war, don't they?"

I nodded.

"Will he live?" she asked.

"I think so. Yes, he'll live."

Then she dropped the subject and would say no more
on the question of either Hunt or the Hessian.

The following morning, I asked Rodney Stephan,
whose fund of knowledge is vast and curious, whether
he thought that the Hessian might have escaped Hunt's
search and made his way southward.

"Southward, Doctor? How far southward?"

"Well, over the Ridge first and into the Hudson River
valley, and then south to York City?"

Rodney Stephan thought about it for a while, and
then he shook his head. "No, sir, Colonel." His titles for
me were many and interchangeable.

"Why not?"

"Hell, Colonel, you know that as well as me—down
there in Westchester's the worst damn place in the
world, you know that. They'll cut your throat for a
shilling, they will, and it don't make one damn bit of
difference what you are, whether you're Tory or Patriot,
they don't give a damn. Hell, no!"

I deferred to his knowledge and thought about it, and I also gave some thought to the fact that the dressing on the wounded boy had to be changed. When I had finished with the single patient I saw in my morning surgery, I had Rodney Stephan saddle my horse, and I rode off to the Heather place. Raymond was cleaning the barn, and he came out to take my horse and to greet me with a query as to whether I preferred black or brown boots.

"Black or brown boots? Why?"

"Well, some will wear only black and some will wear only brown, and some don't care."

"It's a damn curious question, Raymond, and if you are thinking of making boots for me, let me tell you plain out that I will not avoid payment in coin and accept it in kind. You cannot pay me for treating the Hessian. Don't you understand why?"

"I think I do"—Raymond nodded—"but thee are gone to such bitter trouble."

"As you are. And by the way, how is he?"

"Famous—incredibly so."

"Well, he's young and he's strong. Is he still in Jacob's bed?"

"Yes, but fretting to get out and about."

I nodded, and then looked at Raymond long and thoughtfully, until he was constrained to say:

"Is there trouble with me or mine?"

"There will be. There certainly will be. I saw Hunt yesterday. He has the gout. Alice spoke to him, and he told her that when he lays hands on the Hessian, he will try him and hang him. The trial and the verdict together."

"He has the gout," Raymond said. "Poor man."

"Well," I exclaimed, "I will be everlastingly damned

if I understand you people and your half-baked religion! The point is, Raymond, that you must get that boy out of here. And quickly, quickly. Am I right in thinking that three Quaker homes were burned to the ash and one of them right here on Peaceable Street?"

"Ah, now, Doctor Feversham, thee must not think that way, and that was three years ago when feeling ran high, and what did they know, poor devils, who made such a hue and cry about the Friends?"

"Enough to burn down the houses."

"Ah, no. No. Thee overstate the case. These are good folk here on the Ridge and my neighbors."

"They are like any other people, hotheaded, prone to eject reason from any situation, and very obedient and subject to the thinking of Squire Hunt."

Raymond shook his head. "How can I get the boy away? Where can he go?"

"Back onto that British frigate down in the Sound."

"I thought of that. I rode down to Saugatuck yesterday. The frigate is gone."

"You're sure?"

"As sure as my eyes state it."

"Now that's a devil's mess, isn't it?"

"Thee must not fret, Doctor," Raymond said. "God will provide for the lad."

"You're sure?"

"As sure as I am of the ground I stand on."

"Now that's a fair statement of faith, and I envy you, Raymond. We will discuss it. Meanwhile, let me have a look at him."

I moved to enter the house, but Raymond laid a hand on my arm and said gently, "Thee will not give him the feeling that we fear for his presence here or that he is a dangerous burden to us?"

"Good Lord, Raymond, I am not afraid for you and I don't imagine that you are afraid. Hunt will do nothing very awful to you, but if he ever lays hands on him, he intends to hang that boy."

Then I went into the house, and Sarah was sitting by the hearth, nursing the baby; and I stood there, not like a doctor but like a fool, staring at her white breast, and suddenly so speechless and forlorn that she was moved to say:

"Evan, what ails thee?"

I shook my head hopelessly. She rose, handed the child, now asleep, to me, and then hooked her bodice over her breast; and I could only stand and stare at the wet stain of her milk through the dress.

"Is there trouble at home? Is Alice well?"

I forced myself to smile, handing the child back to her arms, and then she placed her in the cradle, telling me, "Thee, Evan Feversham, is the strangest of any man I have ever known, but I suppose that being a Papist and a doctor and a devotee of that incredible game thee call chess all combine to make thee so."

"That's an excellent if somewhat superficial analysis of my character and defects."

She shook her head hopelessly. "Thee mock me, and it be not kind of thee."

"How can I mock you?" I asked her. "I only envy you."

"Ha! What nonsense thee speak! I cook and clean and sew and weave and nurse one child and scold three, and thee has traveled the whole world and been to war and live in a great fine house, and thee is wed to a lovely lady of quality—well, I do not give a fig for thy envy. Thee is very glib, Evan Feversham, but I love thee, and so enough of that. Will thee go up and look at the boy?"

"Did he eat?" I asked, for want of anything else that I could think to say.

"This morning, a bowl of wheatmeal with cream and butter, and two slices of bread and two pieces of bacon and a cup of hot milk and treacle."

"Well—that's encouraging, isn't it?" I said lamely, and she smiled at me and I went up the stairs to Jacob's room, cursing myself for an idiot.

The boy was sitting up in bed, and Sally in a chair beside the bed, and before I came through the open door, I caught a thread of conversation:

"Was thee never afraid?" Sally asking.

"Not when I play the drum. I play the drum and I am *begeistert*. I don't know how to say it in English. But it comes from the drum. I am—"

He broke it off as I entered, starting with alarm. I am six feet tall, and stooping under the low ceiling of the room, I must have appeared to loom over him; but Sally took my hand so eagerly that his fear went with its coming, and she told him who I was.

"Doctor Feversham," he repeated. His English was remarkably good, almost without an accent. "I know. I think about it very much. You save my life, so my life belongs to you."

"Your life belongs to nobody but you, Hans Pohl. And as for saving your life, this lassie here and her father and mother—they saved your life, and enough of that. Let me feel your brow."

His forehead was cool. There was no trace of the fever left. His hair had been combed and washed—by Sally, I learned—and was tied with a ribbon at the nape of his neck. Some color had returned to his cheeks, and he was rather pleasant looking, freckled all over, and with round blue eyes and a wide and comfortable mouth.

"Well, Hans Pohl," I said to him, "you're a lucky lad for the time being. Your fever is gone, and now I'll have a look at your wound, and if it's stopped festering, there's no reason why you can't get out of bed tomorrow. So pull off your shirt and roll over on your stomach."

His arm was lame, and Sally helped him off with his shirt. Her attitude was matter-of-fact, possessive and without any hint of girlish embarrassment. I cut the bandage away, and to my amazement the wound had not only ceased to fester or drain pus, but it had already begun to close. I decided to leave the sutures in for another day, but told him that he could dress that same afternoon and be on his feet.

"Thank you, sir," he said. "I thank you with my whole heart."

"He is all better, truly?" Sally wanted to know.

"For today he'll still be weak. Tomorrow, he can do whatever his strength allows him to do."

"Blessed mercy!" she exclaimed, and then bent over the bed and kissed him with delight. She was a person who did nothing self-consciously or unnaturally, nor had I ever seen in any of her actions any evidence of guilt or shame. The uneasiness was on the part of the boy, but I imagine that my own presence was responsible for that. When he looked at Sally, his expression was as near to worship as I have ever seen on a human face.

"Doctor Feversham," he said to me, "are you a—a Friend, a Quaker?"

"No, I am not."

"Then you will—"

Sally looked at him, smiling, shaking her head slightly, but said nothing.

"No, I will not turn you in," I said flatly and with no enthusiasm. "You are in the house of Raymond

Heather, and to shelter you or not is his decision. I am a physician, and so I keep my own counsel."

"No one will turn you in, Hans," Sally said.

I started toward the door, but the boy stopped me almost pleadingly. "Doctor," he said, "listen, please. I have nobody in the world because my father—" He paused, choked up, and then fought to compose himself. "My father was sergeant," he said, tight and prim now. "By the stone wall, he died with the others. I am— I am afraid," he went on. "I know it is not manly. I know. I did not try to help him. I ran away."

"You could not have helped him. It was too late. He was dead."

He nodded at me, unable to say anything else, and then outside the door, I paused and asked Sally to step out and have a word with me. I took her down the hall to her mother's room and inside, closing the door behind us.

"What on earth are you up to, child?" I demanded of her.

"Do thee think I am a child, Evan Feversham? Look at me. I think I am a woman."

"I have no intentions of arguing the degree of your puberty," I said with annoyance. "I am only trying to drive some sense into that silly pretty head of yours. Don't you bloody Quakers know one damn thing about this war—or any war? War is not a game, not a question of ethics or Christianity—war is a bloody damned insanity. If they take that boy in there, he will not be the first Hessian to be taken by our people. Do you know what hate is? Well, of all the things hated by these bluenosed puritans of yours, and it's quite a list, they hate the Hessians most. I have seen Hessians sold into a lifetime of bondage for thirty dollars and I have seen their women raped with delight, and I have seen Hessians beaten to death. You don't believe me? Well, it's not as senseless as it might appear to be and maybe not as cruel either; it is just an application of that fine old principle, an eye for an eye and a tooth for a tooth. The Hessians cut them to pieces, not once but ten times. The Hessians pinned your Connecticut farm boys up against trees the way a collector pins butterflies, and emptied out their guts too, and many was the belly sprung by a Hessian bayonet that I have pushed the gut back into and sewn up, so the one begets the other, which is always the case when fine civilized, Christian nations decide to solve their problems with mutual murder. They will take it from the English, since they figure that the English have some claim to what we have taken away from them, but they will not take it from the Germans—and that is why, if they take that Hans Pohl of yours, they will hang him up by the neck until he is dead, and that is why this attitude of yours is utterly childish and absurd."

"Have thee finished, Doctor Feversham?" she inquired quietly.

"I am quite finished."

"Yes. And since I have asserted that I am a woman, I will answer thee as a woman answers a man, but with less heat I think, for I honor thee, Doctor, far more than thee appear to honor me."

"For heaven's sake, Sally—" I began, but she went on:

"Please let me speak, for I did not interrupt thee. Thee appear to be an authority on hate, but what do thee know of love, sir? Thee make such a small thing of my love. Not for my life would I offend thee, but why do thee offend me?"

"I did not intend to offend you."

"I am sure thee did not, and I am not taking offense at what thee said of my faith, because thee do not know. Our faith is so simple. Jesus Christ said, Love thy neighbor as thyself, and this we try to do, so where is the great mystery? But my love is not contained. Since I was a child I knew that one day I would love a man. This Hessian is simple and plain and homely. Will thee make it sinful or senseless that I love him? This is where thee offend me."

"Sally, Sally," I begged her, "I am not decrying your sentiments. I know nothing about this boy. I only know that we must get him away from here, and that we must not be hindered by your feelings."

"And do thee think my feelings hinder thee, Evan Feversham? Thee belittle me so. It was I who urged my father to ride to Saugatuck and look for the British ship. But now there is no way to take him away. Is there? Tell me how thee will take him to safety, and see how I hinder thee."

"There must be some way."

"Then when thee know the way, come to us and tell us." And with that, she walked out of the room and back to Jacob's room, and I went downstairs.

Goody Masterson was downstairs in the kitchen when I appeared there. Goody Masterson was past eighty years, but with ears and a tongue as sharp as any twenty-year-old's, and she sewed findings and quilted them into comforters, and goodhearted women like Sarah Heather saved their goose and chicken breast feathers for her. When Goody Masterson saw me, she had to know who was sick and how and why. Perhaps Sarah had hoped I would hear her voice and remain above until she had left; but there I was and nothing to it but to invent a story about Sally.

"Her bleeding!" Goody Masterson snorted. "Why what's wrong with a lassie bleeding? How else is she to bear kids?"

"There is such a thing as enough or too little or too much," I replied.

"And which is it?"

"With all deference, Goody Masterson, I don't think that is for you and me to discuss."

"Indeed! Well, let me tell ye this, Goody Heather," she said to Sarah, "if I had a lassie in her curse, I would not be calling a man. What does a man know? Let me call the midwife, and she does it proper. I will do ye the favor."

"The girl is quite all right," I said.

"And how would ye know with all yer heathen notions to what is under a woman's skirt?"

Sarah soothed her, calmed her, gave her the feathers and took her to the door. Then we stood by the window and watched the old woman plod across the fields.

"So it begins," I said. "The boy cannot stay here."

"She's a harmless old woman."

"With a tongue as sharp as a knife."

"What would thee, Evan? Shall I turn the boy out?"

Back in my own home, I told all of this to Alice, for it was better to have no secrets and no mysteries from her; and she brooded over the question for a while— Sarah's question, "Shall I turn the boy out?"—and then asked me:

"What is the boy like?"

"Well—there's a boy. I've seen a thousand in the army who could be twin to him, not any different from one of your Yankees, middling tall, fair skin, freckled, blue eyes, straw-colored hair. If I were given to that kind of definition, I might say that he has an honest face. He is full of himself right now, for the sergeant who was shot down with the others was his father."

"Oh, poor lad!" Alice exclaimed.

"Well, he who takes up the sword and all that."

"Don't wash it away in clichés, Evan. Do you believe that Sally Heather is truly in love with him?"

"I am not sure that I know what truly in love means."

"I know what it means, Evan. It means the feeling I had the first time I saw you."

"And what was that feeling?"

"Evan—that you should ask me!"

It was ever that way. We would begin and come toward each other and then reach a point and find that it was all dust in our fingers. That the fault and the sickness was mine, I had no doubt. It was always myself who closed the gate, and looking at her now, the pale, lovely face under the black hair, a face alert and intelligent and yearning, I felt a deeper loathing for myself than I had experienced in a long time.

"Evan?"

She called me back to myself. Her annoyance was never very lasting.

I nodded.

"I would like Abraham Hunt and his wife to dinner."

"We've never had them to dinner."

"All the more reason why there should be a first time," she said calmly.

"You know how I feel about him?"

"Of course I do."

"And how he feels about me?"

"Evan," she said, "you have given up with the Hessian boy, haven't you?"

"What do you mean, I have given up?"

"There's no way to save him, so he will die. I don't

want him to die, Evan. If he dies, he will live always between us. Don't you see that?"

I shook my head.

"Well, perhaps you will sometime. It's something I feel deeply, and I think that if Abraham Hunt comes here, we can talk to him about this thing."

"And tell him where the boy is?"

"No, no, no. Of course not. Or even give him any indication that the boy is alive. I don't mean that. I only mean that we might be able to reach out and touch him."

"Reach out and touch Abraham Hunt?" I asked incredulously.

"Evan, Evan, did you ever try to understand us here? How can you and I ever come to each other if you make no effort whatsoever to know who we are? Sometimes, I think you feel we are barbarians. We are not barbarians, Evan, we are plain Christian people who were persecuted and driven for a hundred years before we came to this land, and if we hadn't been hard and narrow and righteous, how would we have endured? You have money and you are a doctor, and my own father was a shipowner, but these are plain, poor people, Evan. Think of what a will it took to scratch a living out of this wretched Connecticut soil, the will that raised up the hundreds of miles of stone wall you see here on the Ridge, and if you think that way about what we were and what we had to become, you might not consider us so rigid and bigoted as you do."

"And you want Abraham Hunt here?"

"Yes."

"All right," I said. "We'll try." Then I reached out and took her hand. "Believe me, I will try, Alice."

Later, we walked together in the garden, Alice and I,

hand in hand, in a good pretense that all was well. Or perhaps all was almost as well as ever it could be. It was one of those lovely May evenings that are like no other time of the year, with the air as sweet as honey and the sunset piling up into awesome layers of pink and violet and gold. When we had built the house, I laid out a garden of paths and hedges to remind me of the gardens in England, and in the time since then Alice had filled the beds with jonquils and lilies and phlox and roses and beddings of every annual she could beg or buy in seed. The jonquils and tulips were with us now, with pale borders of nasturtium, and the lilies thrusting up fat out of the soil not yet in bloom, but still lovely. She was one of those gardeners who knew every plant and bulb and seed too. The garden was her vindication, her refuge, her wall against me and the world and her childlessness, and she took me there tonight as one takes a lover into the innermost recesses of the heart. I had found a bench of alabaster in a dockside warehouse in Philadelphia, when we had turned the place into a hospital. It had been consigned out of Naples to someone in Philadelphia long fled with the British, and the warehouse owner sold it to me for a hundred copper pennies, since hard coin was so rare then, and in due time it was freighted to Connecticut by wagon. That and a marble cupid that I had bought years before in Madrid were the two most precious furnishings of her garden, and I truly believe that she valued them more than any jewels I could have given her. When we sat on the bench, she reminded me of that, and said:

"Do you know, Evan, I always wanted to return in kind, and it had to be a horse, a trained chestnut hunter thoroughbred, of Arab blood and English-trained for fast pacing, and I wait for the war to be over, but I think now that I will wait forever before one can buy a horse out of Britain and have it shipped here."

I did not know what to say, and so I said nothing, and we sat there until darkness fell, and then before we went inside, I said as lamely as a foolish boy:

"You must know that I never touched Sarah Heather, never kissed her, never addressed a single word of affection to her, not a word of what a man might say to a woman—and never will."

"And do you think that makes it better, Evan?"

The following day, I stopped by at the Heather place to take the sutures out of the wound. The boy, Hans Pohl, sat in the kitchen by the hearth, and now he was dressed in Raymond's old clothes and his hair was cropped short in the Quaker fashion. Sally was there, churning butter and at the same time mending his English, trying to rid it of that curious mixture of German and cockney accent that he had acquired among the redcoats, and to instruct him in the high nasal drawl that went for American speech. She was quite clever about it, and I listened with interest for a minute or two before I told him to take off his shirt and let me get at the wound.

It was beautifully healed. I snipped the gut strings and pulled them out, and there was only the slightest ooze of fester. There was no heat on the skin, and I could not help but glow with the neat pride of a surgeon who conquers a bullet.

"How do you feel?" I asked him.

"Good—good. Oh, yes, I feel very good, Doctor Feversham." He paused, then asked, "Can I work, Doctor?"

"Work?"

"He wants to work with my father," Sally explained.

"To pay back," the Hessian said.

I stared at him thoughtfully. "Yes, you can work."

Outside the house, I met Sarah, who was returning from the chicken house with a basket of eggs, the baby in the crook of her arm. She handed me the eggs and set the child down on the grass.

"Can thee use the eggs, Evan?"

"Sarah, our own lay a dozen a day."

"A pity. What can I give thee, Evan?"

"There is no need to give me anything."

"Did thee see Hans?"

"I took the sutures out. He's well now. He tells me he wants to work."

"He's a good lad, Evan, and he says that if he eats our food, he must earn the bread. Certainly there is work enough on the place."

"And where will he stay?"

"Raymond made him a bed in the empty stall. In summertime, it's no hardship to sleep in the barn."

"Sleep in the barn, work in the fields," I said unhappily. "Sarah, you and Raymond are quite out of your minds. How long can it go on?"

"We will lie if we must. If we say he is our nephew, who will say otherwise?"

I shook my head and mounted my horse. "Do this," I told her. "Keep him out of sight at least when people come by."

"Thee is a dear, strange man," she replied, smiling.

The morning after this, I rode over to Redding to set the broken leg of a farmer named Caleb Winters. He had fallen out of the hayloft in his barn, and it was a bad break that involved the ligaments of his knee. He was in deep pain, and I had to feed him half a bottle of rum before I could work on him properly and set the leg. Since it was already late afternoon, I took the short-cut back, through the woods and down to the Norwalk Run, a pretty little stream that rises in the great swamp and flows south into the Sound.

At the edge of the run, I dismounted and sprawled in the grass on the riverside while my horse drank. I was stretched out there, when I saw Hans Pohl and Sally Heather across the stream. They came through a thicket of cattails, walking hand in hand, with no thought or eye for anyone in the world except each other, and then they turned and drifted down along the bank.

My horse came to nudge me and remind me that we were still away from home, but I remained there quietly until the boy and the girl were out of sight.

7

Squire Hunt

SQUIRE HUNT'S WIFE, Abigail, accepted Alice's dinner invitation immediately and graciously. Alice showed me the note Rodney Stephan brought back from their place, and it said:

> *My dearest Alice,*
>   *As ever you have a very special place in my heart, and now that you have done what I cravenly lacked the spirit to do, I shall look forward to the resumption of a friendship once infinitely precious. And most certainly, we accept and will come at the hour you suggest,*
>   *I remain your humble servant,*
>   *Abigail Hunt*

Abigail Hunt was a gracious and well-educated woman, distant kin to her husband, and both of them related to the Cromwells and the Hancocks of Boston. Hunt's father had settled on the Ridge with a gift of the magistracy, but his money came out of the fact that his family held a large interest in the ropewalks in Boston.

He had built the finest house in the neighborhood and sent his son to Harvard College. It was natural of him to marry in Boston, rather than any local girl from the Ridge; and while the *leveler movement* was all over Connecticut—in places with a kind of ferocious fanaticism—I never knew people more respectful of the rich and powerful than these same Connecticut folk. The magistracy of both Abraham Hunt and his father was from the Crown, but no one protested its continuation under the new government. Quite to the contrary, Hunt immediately became the organizer of the local militia, and he led a regiment through the Jersey and Pennsylvania campaign until he came down with a bad case of jaundice that put him on the edge of death for almost six months. He continued to suffer from the liver, perhaps not disconnected with his gout, yet it never subdued his spirit nor quieted a sort of wild violence that always bubbled under the surface of his being.

The day before we expected him, Hunt rode over to the Heather farm, ostensibly to speak with Jacob again, and perhaps in all truth for no other reason; for he never voiced any direct suspicion against Raymond Heather. Sally saw him coming from afar, and she ran to the barn, where the Hessian was cleaning the place as a good housekeeper might clean her kitchen; and then the two of them climbed up into the loft and hid under the hay in the darkest recess of it. As I heard it from Sally long afterwards, it was more of a game and excuse to find themselves together than out of any real fear that Hunt would come poking around the barn after them.

But together they were, body to body and breath to breath, clinging to each other; for even though their hiding thus was a game it was underlined by a deadly reality; and it seems to me that then, in those moments, they faced manhood and womanhood and that awful punishment of maturity, the knowledge that man is mortal and that every moment of his life is fraught with mortality. That Sally had to tell it to me one day is evidence of how poignantly the moment touched both of them. For all that Hans Pohl had lived his life in camp and barracks, he was as virgin as she was, and they clung to each other with fear and excitement, the world exploding into knowledge and joy and terror and that wonderful moment of total insight and understanding that only the first love brings.

Squire Hunt never glanced toward the barn, but dismounted at the kitchen door, and knocked, and was admitted by Sarah, whose heart was racing but who managed to greet him quite calmly:

"A good morning to thee, Squire Hunt, and what would thee?"

His uneasiness troubled her, but I told her afterwards that it was simply the way of any of the Ridge folk when they came into a Quaker place, since it could produce both anger and guilt at one moment—never a comfortable situation.

Raymond ran all the way to the house, Jacob at his heels, and they both entered the house panting; and then there was the family facing Hunt, who apologized for his abrupt appearance and explained that all he desired was to talk to Jacob. I think he was not surprised by their manner, which possibly resembled a group of frightened deer, startled and held transfixed, since he was ready to expect anything at all from those curious people who called themselves Friends.

"About what would thee speak to Jacob?" Raymond asked, realizing now that he had never told Jacob to lie, never told him to dissemble.

"About the Hessian," Hunt replied.

Sarah said simply, smiling, "Sit thee down, Squire Hunt. I would that we could offer thee a small beer or a cup of wine, but it is not our way, as thee know. I have hot water on the hearth and a 'sence of this morning's coffee. It makes a poor drink, but will thee?"

He shook his head. "No, thank you, Goody Heather. Only a word with Jacob. Here, lad," he said to Jacob, "when you saw the Hessians, did you mark the one with the drum?"

Jacob nodded.

"Was he a boy or a man?"

"He was a man," Jacob said evenly.

"How old a man?"

"Sixteen or seventeen years."

"Then he was a boy."

"I will be a man when I am sixteen or seventeen years," Jacob said calmly. "I will do what a man must do."

"By God, you will," Hunt cried. "I like him. He's a damn fine boy, Heather. Was he tall, Jacob?"

"Like a man," Jacob said.

"Well, I suppose that's all I will get out of him," Hunt decided, and then Raymond knew that he should never have doubted his son.

More or less of this was told by Hunt at my dinner table. Abigail Hunt, over the years of being the Squire's wife, had become an apologetic woman. She was essentially a road-smoother, a pretty, dark-haired, dark-eyed version of the laborers who come out in the spring to repair winter ravages to the roads. She repaired her husband's damages and she worshiped him at the same time. Alice considered her to be a well-taught, stupid person, but with this I disagreed. She lived with Abraham Hunt, and managed to remain warm and charming; and she and my wife and a few other women maintained some small form of society in the remoteness and the poverty and the hot summers and long, bleak winters of the Ridge. That in itself required talent as well as patience.

Alice had asked John Dorset, the Congregational minister, and his wife, Ziporah, to join us, since Dorset was one of those lively and imaginative men who fill conversational holes so easily. His wife, Ziporah, was a pale blond lady who had suffered thirty-six years with an impossible name, and nineteen of them with impossible poverty as the wife of a minister on the Ridge; and as a result had been muted into what appeared to be permanent silence, broken only by "Thank you," or "Very nice, I am sure," or some such similar response. Dorset himself had a genial interest in "Popery," as he always called it, and he was by no means a bigoted or arrogant man. If he chose to regard me as a specimen, it was the result of his calling, not of his nature. He was a tall, fine-looking man who, like his wife, was bent by the necessity of being a gentleman and something of a scholar without sufficient finance for either. His wife's linen frock was her single good dress, and with unwitting cruelty both Alice and Abigail Hunt had worn silk. Whatever the local opinion of my religion might be, they regarded me, and without cause, as the only arbiter of what was genteel, and therefore my presence placed burdens on the handful of my neighbors who pursued any type of gentility.

We had made small talk, which Alice directed as carefully as if she walked upon a carpet of shattered glass, until Hunt told the story of his visit to the Heathers; and that raised the question of those curious people who had sought some sort of sanctuary on the Ridge—perhaps because this least inviting part of Connecticut was a place where land could be cheaply purchased—and who called themselves Quakers. They had begun to settle in our rocky valleys and highlands more than half a century ago, and now there were at least twenty families of them among us, with a meetinghouse of their own. They were sober, industrious, decent folk, and they had lived through the years of the war with quiet resignation, accepting the outburst of anger from others and the general climate of contempt with patience and without rancor, an attitude which frequently became more frustrating and annoying to their tormentors than any resistance and anger might have been.

Pastor Dorset pointed out to Hunt that after all, they were God-fearing people, and if they rendered us no assistance, they certainly were of no comfort to the British.

Hunt was in good mood, more relaxed than I had seen him in a long time. We had served up six ribs of seasoned long hung bullock, well roasted, nor had I pricked his guilts with any reference to his gout. He had eaten well, taken three portions of boiled pudding, and washed it down with a bottle of good Portuguese wine; and he was in a mood to give the devil his due. He admitted Dorset's point, but reminded him that at the great battle on the Ridge, they had taken the British wounded into their homes and attended them.

"As they took in our own wounded," his wife reminded him.

"War and charity go poorly together," he said; and

to the minister, "You, John, will disagree with me, but we reason from our calling, don't we? You are a preacher. I am a soldier."

"War without charity is a ghastly thing," Dorset replied. "If we cease to be Christians on the battlefield, then God help us. Don't you agree with me, Doctor Feversham?" he asked me.

"Yes—with some reservation."

"Reservation? I am curious."

"Only that I have never seen evidence of Christianity on a battlefield."

"Not even in your own calling?"

"It comes home in my own calling. You are in a most peculiar position as a surgeon on a battlefield, and trying to repair what grapeshot and musket balls and bayonets have accomplished is hardly an occupation which livens a man's faith."

"I find nothing quite as boring as military talk," Alice said, "and anyway, Abraham, you will admit that the Heathers are pleasant people?"

"They were pleasant enough to me. But damned if I understand people without pride!"

"You find the Heathers without pride?"

"As I consider any man who will not stand up and fight for what is his. I deem it contemptible."

"And you see no virtue in humility?" Dorset asked him.

"Damned if I do! Humility is a claptrap word. When the British come into my land and burn my home and slaughter my stock and ravage my fields, am I to turn the other cheek? A man can't live that way, not without degrading himself."

I couldn't help remarking that the Quakers appeared to live that way without any particular degradation.

Alice caught my eye. I had promised to make no issue with Hunt.

"Do they now? I would say they live in peace and comfort because others were willing to fight their battles. Where would they be if we had bowed our heads as they do?"

"Isn't such a judgment too simple?" Dorset asked.

"I'm a plain and simple man."

"I wish he were as plain and simple when we get into an argument at home," Abigail Hunt said. "He becomes so complex that I cannot follow him at all."

"That's truly characteristic of a husband," my wife agreed.

"But why not become a Quaker if you agree with them?" Dorset asked me, the lack of any sarcasm in his voice indicating that even the Society of Friends was preferable to the Pope.

"I did not say I agreed with them. As a matter of fact, I do not. I simply stated that I find their way of life interesting—and often admirable."

"But how can you think a thing admirable if you disagree with it?"

"I am afraid that, like Squire Hunt, I lack both the courage and the desire to turn the other cheek."

"Courage!" Hunt snorted. "I think it takes damn little courage."

"Ah, now, who is to say?" Dorset put in soothingly.

"And Doctor Feversham," Abigail Hunt said sweetly, "do you think there was ever a cause more just than ours?"

"I thought somewhat about justice when I made it mine," I answered her, and again Alice caught my eyes. I nodded, and pleaded my own position as host.

"Oh, no. No, indeed. You are not let off so easily,

Doctor Feversham. You bully him, Alice," she said to
my wife. "Indeed you do. Don't deny it."

"No one bullies Evan," Alice said quietly, a gentle
knife edge in her voice that no one else at the table
caught. "It might appear so, but truly, no one does."

"Then he must answer my question," she said, with
a kind of simple-minded assurance that I have found
only in well-to-do Boston women. "I asked you, Evan
Feversham, where there was ever a cause more just
than ours?"

"I don't know," I replied.

"You retreat. For shame," she cried.

"No, not at all. I plead ignorance. Perhaps Crom-
well's cause was as just as ours. Or more just. But since
I am a Catholic, I could hardly be expected to look at it
in precisely that light. You see, my dear Abigail, when
nations quarrel, each has a very just cause and God is
always on the side of each."

"My dear Doctor," said Dorset, "your cynicism is
hardly worthy of you."

"I am not a cynic," I replied, suddenly weary of the
whole foolish discussion. "I wish that I were. At least
there's some comfort in cynicism."

"Now hold on here," said Hunt. "Let me put this to
you, Feversham. If you feel as you do, why did you join
our side?"

"I don't see that I've expressed any notion that would
place me on the other side."

"But perhaps on no side," Dorset said.

I shook my head. "No—let me answer you, Squire. I
chose this side for a few obvious reasons, which I thought
you were aware of. For one thing, I married an American girl, whom I care for deeply. For another, my house
stands here, and people sick and hurt in this region are

my patients. For a third, I felt that the British had be-
haved stupidly and abominably, and for a fourth, I am
a Catholic and the British have not been kind to me or
mine. I don't know whether those are reasons enough,
but neutrality is not my nature. I do not admire it."

"Yet your Quaker friends are neutral, are they not,
Doctor?"

"Perhaps. Or perhaps not."

"Pray how are they both?" Dorset insisted.

"Possibly they consider that they are on the side of
mankind."

When they had left, I sat down beside the embers that
remained out of the spring fire, and Alice came and
stood behind a wing chair and stared at me, her expression quizzical and noncommittal. I made my apology.
I had failed her, thereby being rude, argumentative,
disrespectful of a minister of the Gospel, and altogether
a poor host.

"I thought you were marvelously restrained."

"Oh, no."

"Abraham Hunt overeats, belches, and has absolutely
no wit and no sense of humor."

"I thought you were once in love with him."

"Who told you that?" she demanded.

"Abigail."

"Abigail is a stupid cat."

"I think I love you," I said to her.

"You have a remarkably controlled way of demon-
strating it. Also, you are vindictive."

"Am I? In what way?"

"You know he has gout. And you let him stuff himself
with roast beef."

"I am his physician, not his keeper."

"He'll suffer tonight."

"Not from gout. The truth of it is that we don't really know at all what causes gout, and I am not sure it's roast beef. In England people who stuff themselves get gout, and those who are rich enough to stuff themselves are rich enough for roast beef. But you must admit that he refrained from mentioning the Hessian."

"He mentioned the Hessian," she said, rather sadly.

"When?"

"When he kissed me goodnight and got into that ridiculous carriage of his. He said that I should be sure to tell you that as certainly as the Pope sits in Rome, the Hessian will hang."

"He said that! That bastard!"

"You underestimate him, Evan. He isn't stupid."

"Then why do you think he went to the Heather place?"

"I think he went there because he suspected that the Hessian was there."

It rained the following morning, and when it rains people who have put off their ailments to do their plowing and planting come to see me. I had an enormous splinter to cut out of a boy's arm, a case of spring boils, a festering eye, and half a dozen others whose misery I scarcely remember. Not until after our midday food was I able to tell Rodney Stephan to saddle up my horse.

The rain had blown away by then, and the trees in their new green were radiant and jewel-like, and the meadow grass was as straight and high and sparkling bright as if God had just laid it down to make this his own Garden of Eden. I have mentioned that the Ridge has the poorest soil and possibly the most wretched climate in all of New England; but I thought that day, as I had on so many occasions, that it was the most beauti-

ful place in all the world, with its marvelous rock forma-
tions, its sheer cliffs, its numberless little valleys, its cold
lakes and its bright, bubbling streams. In a single mile
of one of its narrow, wretched, twisting roads, there was
an infinite variety of scenery, a deep bog, a high cliff,
a great pile of mighty boulders piled haphazardly as if
some childish giant had played with them and then
heaped them up, and then the meadows, so green and
perfect that one tended to forget what they had been
before these work-worshiping Puritans had taken a mil-
lion stones out of them and built the miles and miles of
stone wall that were the signature of the Ridge country
and a monument that dwarfed some of the incredible
feats of antiquity. If I had been able to explain to Abraham Hunt what came over me when I saw the Ridge
like this in the springtime, he might have been better
able to comprehend why a person like myself had joined
his rags and tatters army to defend this place.

But I was not thinking of Abraham Hunt at that
moment, nor even of the Hessian or the Heathers, to
whose place I was bound, but rather of my wife and the
astonishing and contrary wonder that will happen sometimes between a man and a woman.

Before I reached the Heather place, I came upon
Jacob, on his way back from the meetinghouse, where
the Quakers taught their own children, his round, flat-
brimmed hat perched on the back of his red hair, his
dark, somber clothes at odds with the wordless song of
his own joy that he sang as he hopped and skipped and
ran along.

"Ride me, please, sir, Doctor Feversham," he called
out, and I reached down and swung him up behind me,
finding pleasure in the clutch of his arms around my
waist.

"Oh, what a fine, wonderful horse," he said. "Thee ride the finest horses in the country, Doctor Feversham. My father holds that pacers are a vanity and that God would not will horses to run in any other way than He made them to run."

"I think he is right."

"Then thee flout God's will."

"Unhappily so. I am a sinful man, Jacob. You may do as I say. But never do as I do."

"I don't understand that."

"You will."

We came to the farm, and Jacob took my horse to drink. The child, Annie, was minding the baby, Joanna, the two of them playing in the still-damp grass. Raymond, Sally and the Hessian were nowhere to be seen. I went into the house where Sarah worked at the evening meal, thinking of how unending was the labor of these people from sunup to sundown; and as if reading my thoughts, Sarah turned a face to me so bleak that my whole body tensed.

"What happened?"

She shook her head.

"Is it the boy?"

"Have I no right to be sad, Evan?"

"You are not a sad person."

"Are not all people sad?"

"Don't put me off," I said. "I am your friend."

"Sometimes I wish thee would not come here, Evan. Thee disturb me, and when I am already disturbed, thee make it no better, only worse."

I nodded.

"No, no," she said. "I am being surly, and I repay thy kindness with insolence."

"If you would stop being a damn saint and let your-

self be humanly angry for once, we might both understand each other a good deal better. The Squire was
here, wasn't he?"

"Yes, he was here. Sit down, and I will give thee some
refreshment."

"I want nothing, Sarah, and I did not come for refreshment. I came because it's time for some plain common sense, and because you and I must talk forthrightly,
and because you must stop believing that you Quakers
are alone in a world of beasts."

"Then where are we, Evan?"

"Be damned with where you are! You are here on
the Ridge, and this is the way the world is, on the Ridge
or off it."

"And I feel sometimes that thee swear best and most
in my house."

"I am sorry. I talk my own tongue. I cannot change
it when I come under your roof."

"So now thy anger is all, and thee have beaten me
down. I am unhappy, so thee rage at me."

She stood there at the point of tears. I had never seen
her so reduced, and when I went over to lay a hand on
her arm and comfort her, she suddenly was against me
and I felt the whole surge and warmth of her body. It
was the first time and it was only for a moment, not an
embrace and no reaction after it, only a moment of
two human beings together, and after that she appeared
to be herself again and stepped away and smiled and
poured me a cup of that sorry mixture of burned grain
and old grounds that goes for the name of coffee on the
Ridge.

"I must work or there will be no supper," she said,
going about her chores. "If thee want Raymond, he is

out in the field with the plow. The boy is with him
and Sally went to bring them refreshment."

"I don't want to talk with Raymond. I want to talk
to you. The boy must go. Now. Not tomorrow, not the
next day—but now."

"What has the boy become to thee, Evan?"

"I am willing to take him down to Saugatuck myself.
Then he must make his way to New York as best he may.
We have done what we can do."

"He is not thy care, Evan, but mine and Raymond's."

"Do you know what is happening between him and
your daughter?"

"Is evil happening?" she asked.

"I can't reach you," I said. "So help me God, I can't
reach you in any way."

"Thee reach me, Evan. Truly."

"What happened here with Hunt?"

She told me then.

"And where was the Hessian?"

"He hid in the hayloft with Sally."

"How do you think of Sally? Is she still a little girl?
Or is she a woman?"

"She's a woman, Evan."

"Will you let me take the Hessian away?"

This she did not answer immediately. She sat down by
the table and began to cut through old Swedes. They
were as hard as stone, and I watched the play of muscle
in her strong forearms. Then she looked up at me, her
gray eyes as calm as if nothing in the world could trouble
her.

"We have no churches in our faith, Evan," she said
gently. "We have a meetinghouse, but it is no more
sacred than any other house. My own house is like a

church to me, and if I fail to make it a place where God is, what then have I accomplished?"

I shook my head hopelessly.

"If it is not a place of refuge, then God help me, how can I live here?"

"I don't know," I answered, almost brutally. "I don't know one damn thing about you."

And then I left.

8

The Dog

SALEM ALAN was a Vermont man, who had paused in his wandering on the Ridge because he took a fancy to one of the five Bullett sisters. He was one of those tall, lean, laconic men who cloak dullness in silence, and because he was shiftless and indifferent to most of our "virtues," he was looked down upon, regarded as a thief—for which there was no evidence—and as a poacher, for which there was evidence enough. No one knew very much about his background; he had no kin in the neighborhood; and he said little about anything and nothing about himself. He built a shack in the woods on North Mountain, and he lived on game and what he could get for beaver pelts, when he found them. Then he married Nancy Bullett and they lived on game; and then he fathered five kids who lived as best they could. He never bathed, and generally he was as gamy as a bear a month dead. I was led to his shack once when three of his children were sick, and the smell and condition of the place beggars description.

The only thing he was fond of was his Pennsylvania

rifle, and rumor had it that he had murdered someone
in Vermont for the gun and then fled the country; but in
all probability, he had probably stolen it, since such a
gun was worth ten pounds sterling, and Salem Alan had
never had more than ten shillings in his hand or pocket
at one time. The only thing he appeared to know anything about was hunting, and along with his red setter,
Duklik, after the local Indian chief, he could be found
anywhere and everywhere, prowling after game. In good
times, he killed deer; in bad times, I have heard, his
family would eat squirrels and even fieldmice and weas-
els and crow.

I must mention that he also knew how to train a dog,
and Duklik was the best hunting dog on the Ridge, and
thereby he came into the business of the Hessian. But
I am not much of a believer in accidents, and if it had
not been Salem Alan, it would have been someone or
something else.

He and his dog meandered through the woods, up
from the great swamp for perhaps a mile to the edge of
Raymond Heather's place, and there along the line of
the stone wall that was Heather's boundary. The land
on the other side of the stone wall was Manor land, held
in claim by some absentee landlord in England, but
since the war began, in claim of the Commonwealth of
Connecticut; so Salem Alan was within his right to hunt
there. He stated later that his dog was on deer scent, but
that was simply to elevate the character of the dog, since
the dog abandoned the scent he was on to circle a spot
on the woods side of the stone wall.

Annie, Raymond's little girl, just past four years old,
had drifted all the way to the edge of the pasture, her
play carrying her there, I suppose, without thought or

reason. She had climbed on the wall and was mincing along the top of it, when she saw the man and his dog; and he saw her and guessed that she was one of the Heather children. She came opposite him, and then paused, intrigued by the dog's behavior.

The dog had apparently found a scent and was digging for it. I don't know how to explain this after all the rain we had seen, but I don't know how to explain the senses of a dog either; and as Salem Alan watched on the one hand, and Annie Heather on the other, Duklik dug away at the ground, found what he was after, and pulled back, his teeth locked on the sleeve of the Hessian jacket which Raymond Heather had buried there.

What happened after that is hard to piece out exactly. Evidently the child sensed that something deeply significant was taking place and certainly she was frightened. You would have to understand how thoroughly and confusedly the word *Hessian* had impressed the imagination of every child in Connecticut, and most adults as well, to sense what she felt. There was no placing of right and wrong in her mind, simply a surge of fear that sent her leaping off the wall and racing across the meadow in the direction of her home.

Salem Alan claimed that he did nothing to frighten her or to threaten her in any way, and possibly that was true. He said he called out to her:

"Hey you girl—who are you? What the devil are you running for?"

He swore he did nothing to set Duklik on her, but his dog was certainly sensitive to his voice and alert to his desires. The dog was over the fence in a moment and loping after the child, his long, easy run eating up the distance between them.

Salem Alan insisted that the dog had no intentions of harming the child, that Annie had turned on the animal in terror; and that's as it may be. The man's word was as worthless as the man himself. The result, however, came to me in my surgery in the person of Jacob Heather, who had ridden his father's horse over to my place, and who told me breathlessly that his little sister had been bitten by a dog.

"When?" I demanded.

"Just a while back—as long as it took me to get here."

"Why didn't your father bring her here?"

"I don't know. I think there's trouble over Hans Pohl."

I had already shouted for Rodney Stephan to saddle my horse, and now I threw my instruments into my bag and ran out of the surgery without even waiting for the boy to finish his story. I rode hard, and I don't think it was much more than half an hour between Jacob's appearance and my reaching the Heather place. Raymond and Sally were in front of the house, and I threw my reins to the girl and then followed Raymond into the house.

Annie, her arm swathed in bandages, lay on the kitchen table, over which Sarah had spread a quilt. The child was quite conscious, eyes wide, moist but presently without tears. The baby, who was in her crib, was crying woefully, and Sarah, utterly distracted, turned to me and cried:

"Oh, thank God thee is here—thank God."

"Have you hot water?"

Sarah nodded.

"Then wash my instruments and put them on clean linen. All the needles. Quick now—where do I wash my hands?"

She had soap and a bowl of water waiting, and I washed hurriedly.

As far as the wound in the child's arm went, it was not serious in itself. I had feared to find one of those long, ugly tears that happen when a dog slashes with a will to kill, but here were only four ugly tooth marks, as if the dog had held her while the child struggled to be free and the dog, in response, had increased his pressure and cut through the delicate skin and perhaps a quarter of an inch into the flesh. The bites were bleeding hardly at all.

"Whose dog was it? That's the main thing—we must find the dog."

But neither of them knew, and they could only look at me with voiceless terror.

"Now, look you," I snapped, "for you to lose your minds now and go to pieces over this makes no sense. There's no indication that the dog was mad—"

"But if the dog was mad—" Sarah began, her eyes filling with tears, her voice choking.

"No! Drop that! A mad dog tears, and this is simply a hold on the child's arm." Meanwhile, I had taken my scalpel in hand. "I must cut a bit and make the holes bleed, for only the blood can cleanse it. Not much blood. Don't worry. Did you ask her? Did you try to find out?"

"Who it was," Raymond said, "dug up the Hessian's uniform."

"What!"

Raymond nodded woefully.

"Annie, Annie," I said gently, "you are a brave girl— are you not?"

She stared at me.

"What was the dog like?"

No answer.

"But she told you about the uniform?" I said to Raymond.

"Nothing else."

"Was the dog's mouth white? Tell me, Annie." I took a silver shilling out of my pocket. "You shall have this. A whole silver shilling. You can buy a doll at Miss Crocus' shop in Norwalk. And not a rag doll either. A fine doll with a silk dress and real hands and real feet. But you must be a smart girl and answer me."

Her eyes were fixed on the coin. She smiled slightly.

"Did you ever watch your father shave?" I asked her.

"Yes," she whispered.

"You know how he makes a lather out of soap and puts it on his face? Do you know what I mean?"

"Yes."

"Did the dog have white soap on his face? Now think, darling. You must answer truthfully, and then I will give you this."

She struggled for the memory, and then the tears came. I took out a second shilling. "For two shillings," I said quietly, "you can have the finest doll in Connecticut."

"No," she whispered.

"You mean there was no soap on the dog's face?"

She sat up now and nodded.

"Good girl. Oh, you're a wonderful girl, Annie. I think I would give anything to have a little girl like you. Indeed I would. Now you must think again. Was there soap in the dog's mouth?"

"It was a red dog."

"Wonderful! Now isn't she a fine girl? Isn't she, Sarah?"

"She is—she is," Sarah said, trying to hold back her own tears.

"But did he have soap in his mouth?" I insisted. "Was there foamy soap dripping from his mouth?"

"No, he was a red dog."

"Damned if I don't think it Salem Alan's beast." I put the two coins in her hand. "Hold tight on these, and I must prick your arm a little. Oh, just a little."

A few minutes later, the cuts were clean and her arm was bandaged, and I had decided that it was hopeless to rage at Raymond for burying the uniform when he could have burned it or hidden it somewhere in the house. Sarah had retreated into a corner where she let herself sob out her terror against the wall. I could understand that, what it meant to look at a live child who is already dead, for there is no recovery from a rabid dog. She was herself again when I finished with Annie, and then I said to Raymond:

"The dog was not mad, and the odds are that I am right and it was Salem Alan's dog, and if that's so, how long do you think it will be before they are here? Where is the Hessian?"

"He hides in the hayloft."

"What!" I exploded. "Are you out of your mind?"

"Where else can he hide?"

"You fool," I thought, and then I realized that he and Sarah were both half out of their minds with the belief that their child had been bitten by a mad dog, and there was no blame to them.

"All right. We must get him out of here. Saddle your horse, Raymond, and I'll lead him down to Norwalk and work out something, somehow. I don't know what, but I will think of something."

I don't know what I would have thought of. If I had taken him down to Norwalk, I might have paid someone to take him through Westchester or found a boatman to sail him over to Long Island; but even then who knows that the outcome would have been so different? But it was too late already. Raymond opened the door, and there was Sally staring at Squire Hunt and half a dozen of his militiamen riding up to the farm.

In answer to Sally's wordless, terrified question, I said, "You do nothing, Sally—and don't go to the barn. Believe me, there's no way out now unless a miracle happens. But I don't want the boy hurt or shot, so both of you be still and let me talk to Hunt."

It was midday now, cool, quiet except for the even beat of the horses' hoofs, a gentle, sunny day in May—a day of the kind of sweet charm that appears to embrace tragedy; and I remembered such a day when my father was buried and the graveyard a garden of beauty, old roses and green, sweet-smelling grass.

They dismounted. One of them held the horses. The rest followed Hunt as he strode up to me and greeted me. No anger now. He had won and we had lost, and he was magnanimous.

"Good day, Feversham. What brings you here?"

"A dog ripped their child's arm."

"I'm sorry to hear that."

"Was it Salem Alan's dog?"

"Apparently. He said it only nipped her in play."

"He is a lying son of a bitch." He was the man who held the horses, and I said it loud enough for him to hear. "Was the dog rabid?"

"No, no," Hunt replied comfortingly, and then without turning, "Tell them how healthy your dog is, Salem!"

"No, Doctor Feversham—" Alan began, and I cut him off sharp with:

"I'll hear nothing from you, Alan! Just shut your damn mouth!"

"Well, I like your manner, Feversham. I always have."

"What do you want here, Hunt?"

"Is that for you to ask?" He drove a finger at Raymond. "Or for him?"

"What do thee want?" Raymond asked quietly.

"Oh, what do thee want?" one of Hunt's men repeated lispingly, mimicking Raymond.

"You know what I want," Hunt said. "I want the Hessian. I know he's here, and I'll find him if I have to pull your place into pieces."

"Suppose I said he isn't here," I put in.

"Don't be a fool, Feversham. I have had a notion he's here for days now. Now I have the proof." He walked back to his horse, lifted the flap of his saddlebag, pulled out Hans Pohl's dirty uniform coat, brought it back and flung it at Raymond's feet. It lay there a moment, surrounded by a silent tableau; and then Sally picked it up, walked over to Hunt and said to him:

"Take this and get out of here, sir. This is our land, and thee has no place here."

Hunt took the coat, passed it to one of his men and nodded with approval at Sally. "Well spoken. But it's pointless. Will you tell her that it's pointless, Feversham?"

I walked over to Sally and she met my eyes, and I shook my head. "Don't let them hurt him, Evan," she whispered.

"What will you do with him?" I asked Hunt.

"You know what I will do with him, Feversham. We're not going to beat him or torture him. We'll lock him up, and when General Packenham gets here, we'll hold a

trial. Now understand me"—he came close to me then
and spoke quietly—"I want no trouble with the
Heathers. There are those who hate the Friends, I don't.
I have no love for them, no hate for them. They are
here, and that's it. What these people do, they do out of
their own way. They are not enemies and neither are
they ours, and for my part I don't give a damn what
they are. I want the Hessian, and there's no one here who
can stop us from taking him."

I nodded.

"Where is he?"

"I have your word for what you say—as between
us, Hunt, as between two men who have respect for each
other?"

"Yes."

I walked away from him then and to Sally, and took
her a few paces away, and I said to her, "You must bring
him out, Sally."

"No—oh, no, please, Evan."

"They will not hurt him. They will take him away
and lock him up and then he will be tried. We did what
we could, Sally. We did all that we could."

"They will kill him."

"No. They are going to try him in a court. Believe
me—I promise you nothing, but Squire Hunt will not
hurt him now. So go to him and make him understand
that he must give himself up."

"Oh, my God."

"You must do it, Sally, because there is no other way."

For a long, long moment, we stood facing each other;
then Sally turned and walked off toward the barn.

"Where is she going?" Hunt demanded.

"She's going for the boy. He's just a boy. In God's

name, will you remember that he's just a boy, Hunt?"

Hunt made no reply, and we stood there and waited. Inside the house, the baby, Joanna, had stopped crying. The door opened, and Sarah appeared, herself again, the broad, lovely face calm under the mass of her honey-colored hair. She walked over to Raymond, took his hand and stood next to him.

No one moved, no one spoke. Time passed, and finally Hunt said to me, "Oh, I do dearly hope you're not playing a game with me, Feversham."

"You see the barn," pointing to it. "The girl went in there. The boy is in there. Where could they go? You'll have him long enough, Hunt. Be patient."

"Squire Hunt?" Raymond said.

Hunt turned away from the barn to face him. I don't know what was in Hunt's mind then, nor did I ever understand either his need for the conquest of the Hessian or his apparently malignant hatred of the Hessian, so much was he alien to me; yet at that moment he appeared to turn toward Raymond with a sort of pity; and to give the devil his due, he never raised the question of any punishment directed toward Raymond or myself —perhaps because he sensed the quality of our own anguish.

"What need thee the boy," Raymond asked, "when all the rest of his company have died and paid the price? His own father was in the company and he perished. He is a good boy. He works hard—"

I don't know where Jacob was until then. Perhaps he had hidden somewhere out of his own fear of Hunt and what Hunt might do; but now the boy appeared around the house and went to his father, standing close to him. Raymond paused, looked down at his son, and then lifted a hand to touch the boy's hair gently. I was deeply moved at this. Raymond was neither a demonstrative nor a very articulate man, and I knew what it cost him to speak thus to Hunt.

"Go on," Hunt said, neither coldly nor warmly. No one mimicked Raymond now. The militiamen, silent, forbore to look at him.

"I will take him in for my own," Raymond pleaded. "Others have bought Hessian prisoners into bondage. If thee will, I pay thee up to the whole value of my worldly goods and give thee mortgage on my home and fields. If thee desire him punished, I will punish him. Only leave him here with me."

"That cannot be," Hunt said, a note of weariness in his voice. "I will not argue it, Heather. He hanged Saul Clamberham, who had done him no wrong."

"Not him! His officer!"

"I will not argue it, Heather!"

What had transpired between Hans Pohl and Sally Heather in the barn during all of this, I don't know and most likely will never know. Most of my own youth I have forgotten, and purposely, for it was not worth the remembering; but the taste of my first love, when I was no older than this Hessian boy, I will never forget as long as I live, for it was one of the few moments in my life when I knew that God existed and that the world was filled with ecstasy; and this I thought of when I saw them come out of the barn, the girl suddenly like her mother, not a girl any longer but a woman of beauty and dignity, her head held high, and the boy next to her holding her hand and walking straight and proud.

Not a sound now, not from any of the militiamen, not from Raymond or Sarah or their children. Sally and the boy walked over to where the militiamen were. One of them took a piece of rope and tied the boy's hands behind his back, and then they lifted him into the saddle, so that he rode double with a militiaman behind him. And then Abraham Hunt mounted his horse, and the rest of them mounted, and they rode away.

9

General Packenham

"ARE YOU AWAKE?" my wife asked me.

I had thought her long asleep. I lay on my back, which is a surrender to sleeplessness, and I had thought that half of the night was already gone by.

"Yes, I am awake."

"You were awake last night. Try to sleep."

"If I were asleep, I would not be awake, and if I could sleep, I would sleep."

"Does your wound hurt?"

It always hurts, and I was used to it, and that was not what kept me awake.

"Do you think about death when you can't sleep, Evan?"

"Sometimes."

"Are you afraid?"

"Sometimes—yes."

"Do you believe in God, Evan?"

"At times."

"I no longer ask you to be baptized in our church—"

"I have been baptized, as you may recall. As wretched as Catholics are, they still baptize their children."

"Evan, I didn't mean it that way. I used the word baptize—you know what I meant. Why do you become so cold and cruel? I only meant to comfort you, and I don't know how."

"I am sorry. Forgive me."

She was silent for a while then, and I asked myself, as I did so often, why I had to hurt her in a world that already had sufficient hurt and hatred—and I found no answer. And then she said:

"I was with Abigail today."

"Oh? Were you?"

"I go and you don't care where I go."

"I knew you were gone. Must I dog you to know every place that you go?" There was silence again, and I said to her, "I don't know how to be alone anymore. Don't you think I feel it when you go?"

"Thank you, Evan," she whispered.

"What did Abigail say?"

"That her husband doesn't listen to her, that he hasn't heard a word she said for more years than she cares to remember."

"Yes."

"You know what she means?"

"Yes, I sometimes think that we have stopped listening, all of us."

"Still I begged her to talk to him."

"Will she?"

"She says that it's his burden now."

"What is?"

"The Hessian boy."

"She calls it a burden? The man is compelled. Well, maybe it's a burden. He lives in his own hell."

"Do you understand why he wants the boy's life?"

"I understand," I said. "There's no other way for

Abraham Hunt to live. What is right is right. What is wrong is wrong, and above all he's a righteous man, isn't he?"

"I don't know what you mean by that."

"I mean it plainly. He's a just man."

"Then are you a just man, Evan?" she asked after a long moment.

"No. I don't know what justice is."

"You don't mean that."

"I mean it."

"Then I don't understand it. Do you know what Abigail asked me? She asked me whether they had lain together."

"Who?"

"Sally and the German boy."

"She's a slut!"

"Who?"

"Your friend, Abigail. Your friend, Abigail, is a slut."

"What a thing to say!"

"A very natural thing."

"She had compassion. She had compassion for the poor girl. What if the girl carries the child of the Hessian? Is that any reason to call Abigail a slut?"

"Yes—damn good reason!"

"It's always this way when we talk. It always comes to this. No matter how I desire to be together with you, I can't, I can't."

She said no more, and I lay there with my eyes closed, and in time I felt her body gently against mine, and then I slept.

The next day, Raymond Heather brought Annie to my surgery, and I changed the dressing on her arm. I had meanwhile seen the dog, Duklik, and satisfied myself that he was not rabid; and when I exposed the wound, I saw that the bite was healing rapidly and cleanly, as is so often the case with children.

"How is Sally?" I asked him.

"Somber. She keeps her peace."

"Have you tried to talk with her?"

"Yes, I've tried."

"And?"

He shook his head. "Will they hang the boy, Doctor Feversham?"

"I don't know."

I asked the same question of Rodney Stephan the day after that, and he replied without hesitation, "They surely will, Doctor."

"How do you know?" Of course, it was a meaningless question, because Rodney Stephan knew everything that took place on the Ridge, and the quality of his knowledge was something he could not explain.

"It's about. It's surely about."

"And they're not satisfied with the slaughter that took place."

"It was a bellyful of slaughter, it was, like a hog killing. But a Hessian's a Hessian, and he watched the murder of Saul Clamberham."

"And when will they hold the trial?"

He knew that too. General Packenham would arrive during the next day or two, and then the trial would be held. I remembered Packenham only too well. I had been at Saratoga when he had his quarrel with Colonel Stark and when Stark had been close to killing him in his anger at what he felt was Packenham's cowardice, and had finally been content to humiliate him. Packenham was a vain and pompous man, well-fleshed with an imposing manner and a florid complexion. He was one of those men in whom nature and overeating combine to produce an aspect of substance and authority, a large head, a great beak of a nose, and a deep, rasping voice.

His command in this area was a tribute to the fact that the war had gone elsewhere; but the fact that he would preside at the trial gave me no great hope for the boy; and when I told Alice who he was and what we might expect from him, she asked me who would defend Hans Pohl.

"I don't know," I admitted. "I had supposed that Packenham would bring a defense with him from New Haven."

"And if he did, after what you tell me of Packenham, what difference could it make?"

The next day, my patients were full of the news that General Packenham and his aide, Colonel St. August, had arrived in town and had taken rooms at the inn. I recalled vaguely the name of St. August, perhaps in relation to some court-martial or perhaps in connection with the Adjutant General, but nothing definite that I could call to mind. The talk I heard was for the most part of their splendid uniforms, for the best that we on the Ridge had ever put together in the way of uniform was eight blue coats with sashes for the leaders to wear in militia parades. If St. August was for the defense, then who would prosecute? I somehow felt that Abraham Hunt would avoid the post, for not only was he the local magistrate but his victory would be cheapened if he got it by the force of his own personality. Also, he would be one of the main witnesses, which would put him in a rather embarrassing position.

Again, this night, Alice asked me who would defend the boy.

"I don't know. Possibly St. August."

"Everyone says he's the prosecutor."

I shook my head hopelessly.

"Would you defend him, Evan?"

"Do you want me to?" I asked incredulously.

"I don't know what I want. I don't know what side I am on—if there are any sides here, and I don't know what the right or wrong of it is. Did you save his life?" she asked.

"No, of course not."

"I meant with his wound."

"The wound healed itself. I helped him. I did what I could—but if you're thinking that I could defend him now—no. It's impossible."

"Why is it impossible?"

"I'm a doctor, not a lawyer."

"You're a colonel in the army. You still have your rank. You led a regiment. Certainly you are peer to Mr. St. August. Why could you not defend him?"

"No," I insisted. "It's wrong. He must have a lawyer."

"And do you think they'll find him one? The trial is tomorrow. Do you really think they'll find him a lawyer?"

So it was that an hour later, I knocked at the door of Squire Hunt's house. Abigail opened the door herself, surprised and patently pleased to see me, and making her small joke about a household in perfect health.

"Yet I am sure the Squire will be delighted to see you," she said. "You are always more welcome in health than illness, Evan."

"He's here?"

"In his study with General Packenham."

She led me through the sitting room into the study. Theirs was a fine and well-appointed house, the fireplaces framed in white Italian marble, the woodwork full of scroll and leaf patterns, the sidechairs imported

from England and the floors of polished hardwood
rather than the pine that was generally used for flooring
in the neighborhood. The study had a wall of calf-
bound books which, read or unread, gave the place an
aspect of culture and civilization.

Abigail knocked and then entered at Hunt's bidding,
introducing me as if it were the most natural thing in
the world for me to turn up at the Squire's house un-
announced in the hour of twilight. Both the men were
taken somewhat aback. Hunt introduced me to Packenham as Colonel Feversham.

"Ah, a colleague. Always pleased to meet a patriot,
honored to, Colonel," Packenham said, thrusting out a
meaty, wet hand to clasp mine. He squinted at me.
"Haven't we met before?"

"At Saratoga, General."

"Oh? Were you with Gates?"

"No, sir." I hesitated; I could not help myself. Hunt
was watching me narrowly. "I was with Stark."

The General stared at me coldly. "Are you a Ver-
monter, sir?"

"I am English," I replied. "I led the Eleventh Connecticut Volunteer Riflemen—or what was left of them,
only thirty-two men. So they put me with Stark."

The General nodded brusquely. "I see."

"Feversham here is a physician," Hunt said, sensitive to the bleak distaste in Packenham's expression. "I
spoke about him. He tended the Hessian's wound."

Packenham cleared his throat. "I see. In other words,
this is the man who took it upon himself to shelter and
heal and give aid and comfort to a malignant enemy of
our cause."

"I sheltered no one, General," I said quietly. "As for
healing and aid and comfort to the enemy, I have per-

formed that same function on many battlefields and I have yet to be reprimanded for it."

"Then perhaps the time is at hand, Feversham. Arrogance has its fall, hasn't it? The Squire tells me that with every loyal militiaman hunting this Hessian, you laughed up your sleeve with the knowledge of who he was and where he was. And yet you walk in impunity. I would not sleep well or easily, if I were you. Who knows whether this trial might not be broadened?"

"Are you threatening me, sir?"

"Informing you, sir."

"I don't threaten, I don't inform," I said very softly. "But I must remind you, General, that I was very close to Colonel John Stark. We were much like brothers. I also have in my desk at home a personal letter from General Washington, thanking me for the reorganization of his medical service, and begging me to call upon him if the need be. I may add that I am still a part of a commission for hospitals, headed by Doctor Benjamin Rush, who is a friend of mine and also a member of the Congress. I simply cite this so that when you make your threats—"

"I make no threats!" he interrupted me.

"Good. I assume we both dislike threats. Now if I may take up my business with Squire Hunt?"

"As you please, sir."

Hunt, who was watching this byplay with interest, nodded at me and said, "Go on, Feversham. I am listening."

I was neither complacent nor proud of myself, and indeed my behavior reminded me of the behavior of a small, petulant boy; nor had I done anything to help the Hessian. I had antagonized General Packenham perhaps beyond apology, for I had called to mind not only his own cowardice but the humiliation he received at the hands of Colonel Stark, and I had placed Hunt, who might have been neutral, upon the defensive. My falling back upon the security granted by a relationship with famous personalities was a bluff and a lie—something Packenham might never know, but something I knew full well and would have to live with as I lived with so many other small shames. I was like a brother to Stark for one day in the heat of combat, and I doubt that now he even remembered my name. My letter from General Washington was one of hundreds of similar letters, and of as little moment; and as for my relationship with Dr. Benjamin Rush, while I had been appointed to a commission by him, I had never met him, nor had the commission ever sat. My claim to his friendship was a lie, concocted by a sudden fear that Packenham might persuade Hunt to put me and the Heathers on trial with the Hessian; and while subsequent reflection showed me how ridiculous such a notion was, my own panic, disguised by a calm and quiet voice, led me into the flood of counterthreat and falsehood.

I was not proud of myself, not by any means, and I said to the General now, "Forgive me for my show of temper, sir."

Hunt watched with acute attention. He had never heard me apologize for anything before. Packenham nodded stiffly, and I said to Hunt, "While the General here, Squire, has ample credentials to sit as military judge and prosecutor—"

"Colonel St. August will sit with me as prosecutor," Packenham interrupted.

"As prosecutor," I said. "But who will defend the Hessian?"

"The court will defend him," Packenham replied.

It was not unheard of, and I could recall precedent I myself had seen; but never where the court consisted of two officers only, and now I asked who else would sit on the court. Would Squire Hunt sit on the court?

"He is chief witness, as I understand it, sir."

"Then only yourself—"

He interrupted me again. "I do not understand your concern, Colonel Feversham. As I have heard this case described, there appears to be no reason on earth why justice cannot be swiftly and competently done. Do you doubt my ability to conduct a just court?"

"No, sir."

"Do you come here to plead for the Hessian?"

"I came because I believe that a military lawyer should sit and defend."

Packenham shrugged. Hunt said nothing.

"Would you allow me to sit on the court?" I asked.

"You, sir," Packenham replied, "are even more involved than Squire Hunt, who is at least the commander of your local militia. I know of no command you hold, sir. Have I been misinformed?"

"I hold no command."

"Then I suggest, Mr. Feversham"—dropping any title now—"that you have faith in the cause I represent and in the uniform I wear."

I turned to Hunt, pleading silently.

"There is nothing I can do, Feversham."

"Would you allow me at least to talk with the boy, to advise him, to help him with his defense?" I begged of Packenham.

"What boy, sir? What boy do you refer to?" He was becoming increasingly sure of himself, increasingly pompous as my own position became plainer and weaker.

"The Hessian, Hans Pohl. He is only a boy of sixteen years."

"What kind of talk is this, sir? Have you never seen boys of sixteen, fifteen, fourteen even in our own ranks? Have you never seen them lying dead, having paid the highest price a lad can pay?"

"Still, that doesn't change the fact—"

"I know one fact, Mr. Feversham. The man is a Hessian. He wore a Hessian uniform and he took Hessian pay. He killed for hire."

"God damn that," I cried. "Every soldier who ever set foot from a ship onto our soil killed for hire—Hessian, British, French, Scot! What damn difference does it make? They all kill for hire! This whole filthy game is played for hire! I'm only asking you not to make us like them, to show some Christian mercy!"

"Christian mercy?" Packenham asked, raising one brow. "How curious from you, sir! I had not known that you came over to our faith. I had heard that Rome was your first allegiance."

"You stinking, cowardly bastard!" I said, and I turned on my heel and left the place.

10

The Trial

WHEN ALICE AND I arrived in the village on the morning of the trial, we found a great crowd assembled in front of the tavern, which is on the main street and the first building of any consequence as one enters the town. There must have been two or three hundred people in front of the place, and I recognized faces from Redding and from Danbury and even from Salem over in York State. Others, I am sure, rode all the way up from Saugatuck and Norwalk, all hoping to get into the big pipe room, which at best could hold no more than fifty and those packed in tight enough.

I do not blame them. Little enough happens on the Ridge, from season to season, that might be called an event. Indeed, once winter sets in, the Ridge can be the most isolated place in the world, and spring brings its own excitement, its own opening up; and here in this late and lovely springtime was that fiercest of all drama, a man on trial for his life, and not just any man but that most hated of all men in those strange years we lived

through, a Hessian. Perhaps it was our own sad fate that
the war had moved so far away from us, for with all the
cruelty and imbecility of battle, one's own involvement
in it brings out not only the worst in men but often
enough the best in them, and with the mercilessness
comes mercy too. Here the enemy was a single man who
was no man at all, but a poor orphan lad thousands of
miles from home. But that mattered not at all, and the
fact that hardly more than a fortnight had gone past
since the fight at Naham Buskin's farm did not make
for much pity for the single survivor.

Not that people called for blood; it was not the way
of these people, except for a handful of loafers who are
found in any community. These were a deeply religious
and proud and reticent people, whose God was just and
unforgiving, who not only read the Old Testament but
who lived it too, who named their children after the
same ancient people whose prayers they recited, whose
grandfolk had come into a wilderness and tamed it and
driven out the Canaanites, who were red men but
Canaanites too, and who lived by the letter of the justice
they professed, an eye for an eye, a tooth for a tooth.
They were not a frivolous people; what was good was
work, and work was good. Yet they were not without
toleration and some comprehension of a necessity for
difference. The Quakers lived among them in peace,
unharassed, and while they had driven out the Tories,
they had not murdered them. If a hard and puritanical
God inhabited their churches, the doors of their churches
remained open to anyone, and when John Dorset saw me,
he came to me as if the single outsider must be per-
suaded. Yet his own argument came first.

"I can do nothing," he said. "What can I do?"

I would not ease his conscience or answer his question.

"The trial will be just. I spoke to Packenham."

"All trials are just," I agreed.

Alice found Raymond and his daughter Sally. Sarah had remained at home with the children. Only Raymond had been called as a witness, and as he told me, Sally would not stay away but insisted that she come with him. I wondered about that, and whether this was anything she should see.

"I must see it," she said. "Try to understand that I must see it, Evan. Don't question me now."

Abraham Hunt came through the milling crowd and found us, and he was curiously gentle. He had put on his militia uniform, his blue coat and white trousers, and he wore a wig and a wide sword sash, the small sword hanging incongruously from his big figure. He was not at ease in his uniform. At least a hundred men and boys from the Ridge country had gone off to the war at one time or another, and not one of them had ever worn a uniform, and I think that Hunt remembered this in terms of what would come up at the trial. Also, his uniform fitted him poorly, for we had no tailors on the Ridge and sewing was done at home. I noticed Colonel St. August pushing through the crowd to enter the inn. He was a tall, slender, youngish man, and he wore a brown coat with yellow facings, the uniform of an artillery regiment that he had organized somewhere in northern Connecticut. He was said to come from a wealthy family and had paid out of his own pocket for two five-pounder cannon, but whether his company or cannon had ever done more than parade, I do not know. The colonies were full of eager men of wealth and social position who had designed beautiful uniforms and organized companies of their own, but somehow one rarely remembered them from a battlefield.

Hunt greeted Raymond, not ungraciously, and asked where the boy, Jacob, was.

"At home," Raymond said.

"But he must testify."

"There was no warrant for him," Raymond said. Raymond still did not know his own status, whether he would be punished, whether he would join Hans Pohl at the dock, whether he would be made to stand in the stocks, day and night, in the peculiar agony of that singular Puritan punishment that they so cherished in New England and which they had applied to so many of his faith when the war first began. I had begun to appreciate how different Raymond's response to the affair was from mine. If he had no courage compounded out of hatred and anger, neither did he have the sickly inner fear that went with such courage. Somewhere inside of him, there was an ultimate calm and acceptance, so unaggressive that it could easily be mistaken for cowardice, as so frequently it was. He was a small man, small-boned, but he stood straight, for all the years he had spent over his cobbler's bench, and with the knee-length, somber Quaker coat buttoned up to his neck, he had great dignity and self-possession. I have noticed that the Quakers wore clothes that appeared always to be ten years behind the current style, and since the style on the Ridge was usually about ten years behind what it was in the cities, the Quakers had an antique look about them—very much like the appearance of those Jews I have seen on occasion in Europe, clad in their long black coats and wide-brimmed hats, with their strange beards and side curls, but walking straight with a kind of inner knowledge, as if they were kings in their own right and inner being; and that was the way the Quakers were, full of an inner sufficiency that could be as irritating to strangers as bad manners and arrogance. Yet it was neither bad manners nor arrogance, but rather the other side of the coin.

At least a dozen Quaker men were outside the inn, keeping close to Raymond but behind him, all of them grouped, the sameness of their dress like a uniform, their coats buttoned high in spite of the heat, their round hats straight upon their heads, unsmiling but neither hostile nor afraid, only there with their presence. None of them were let into the inn, and later in the day they were gone. I had assured myself that I, at least, had great intimacy with the Heather family, but now I realized how little I knew of them or their way of life or their thoughts or their religion, and I was struck with the fact that here they were a fragmented people within a people, an island within an island, folk who had not come to this place with hard anger and grim courage, gun in hand, to wrest it from the savage and the wilderness, but in a sort of nakedness—and as a moment of insight will break through a person's dullness, so did I comprehend suddenly what love meant to Sally Heather, and I felt myself full of a kind of melancholy I had not known before.

Perhaps Alice felt something of the same, for she took her place on the other side of Sally as Hunt told Raymond, "Then you must go for the boy, Heather. I am sorry, but we must have him here."

Raymond nodded and went off, leaving Sally with us, and then Hunt cleared a way through the crowd to the inn. They gave way for him, with his cronies beseeching him for a place, as if it were a cockfight; and then we went out of the sunlight into the crowded taproom, already so full that it appeared impossible that anyone else could be squeezed in.

Yet somehow, an open space was maintained in the middle by four militiamen, who wore blue coats and crossed white belts, and who kept pressing the crowd back. At one end of this space, a long table had been set up, and behind the table were seated General Packenham, Colonel St. August, and Bosley Crippit, the town clerk and recorder, with pen and ink and a sheaf of paper in front of him. There were chairs on one side of the open space, and here already seated were Miss Perkins, the schoolmistress, Mr. Saxon, the undertaker, and Salem Alan. I guessed that the Hessian was held in some other room in the inn, in the kitchen or the pantry; and this was the case.

For a little while, the confusion continued. At least a dozen men were ejected forcibly, and the air was full of arguments, name-calling and catcalls—and in one case an actual scuffle between the militiamen and someone who claimed he had ridden all the way from New Haven to see the thing. Writers from three newspapers complained that they were put where they could see nothing of what would happen, and others fought for better places, so it was at least fifteen or twenty minutes after we had entered before some kind of order and silence was achieved out of the drumming of Packenham's gavel upon the table.

Hunt had placed the three of us, Alice, myself and Sally, across the open space from the witnesses, finding a bench on which we could sit, but most of those present sat on the floor or stood with their backs against the walls, and outside the windows were crowded the faces of those who could not enter. The air was thick and heavy, and so little light entered the place that the whole proceeding went on in a sort of gloomy twilight.

Having achieved a sort of order, Packenham asked

the witnesses to identify themselves. There was little form or exactitude about courts-martial in those days, each presiding officer setting the rules more or less as he pleased, with no appeal and no rein on his actions. Here Crippit read the names of the witnesses, and each one stood for identity. I was named as a witness, as I half expected I would be, even though I was never served. Sally was not named. When the clerk came to Raymond's name and there was no response, Packenham said with irritation:

"Why is he not here, Squire Hunt? I warranted him. Why was no subpoena served upon him?"

"There was no need to be that formal. He was here. I sent him back for his son."

"Formality is the nature of things military, Squire," Packenham said. "When will he be here?"

"Within the hour, I am sure."

Crippit handed Packenham a paper, and the General complained about the light.

"Why are there no candles?" St. August demanded. "The place is black as a pit."

"It's bright daylight," said Oscar Latham, the innkeeper, and half the audience burst into laughter.

"It is not bright daylight, Innkeeper," Packenham said. "Bring us a dozen candles."

Muttering about who was going to pay for them, Latham pushed his way through to the kitchen, and the proceedings waited until he returned with a lighted candle in one hand and a bundle in the other, which he reluctantly lit and distributed around the table.

"With light comes justice," St. August observed, his voice piping and nasal, with a Boston accent he either came by naturally or affected.

Packenham smiled tolerant and tapped with his gavel

again. I glanced at Sally, who sat primly and erectly, her hands folded in her lap, apparently oblivious to the eyes directed upon her, the grins and the whispering. Gossip had dealt with her swiftly and cruelly, and from the moment she appeared in front of the inn, the looks cast upon her took on that subtle and wretched connotation that goes with public exposure of any relations between a boy and a girl that can be visualized as sinful.

"We will come to order," Packenham announced. "I hereby convene a military court in the name of the Sovereign State of Connecticut and the Continental Congress."

"General Jonah Packenham presiding," Crippit called out, "with the commission of the military council of the state. Colonel Albert St. August sitting with him. These are summary proceedings under a state of war. The accused is one Hans Pohl, a soldier in the army of the Elector of Hesse and sworn to action under the flag of King George the Third of England."

Bosley Crippit was in his glory, and I could imagine the hours he had spent putting together the pompous and ridiculous phrases that made up the charge. He was a potbellied little man with a shining, hairless skull now hidden under a massive wig. The wig was his pride and joy, imported from Paris, and he never tired of telling how he had ordered it, via London and Philadelphia for six guineas. In all his years of writing and rewriting the details of land titles and boundaries, he had never had such an opportunity as this, and he was making the most of it. Yet the fact that the trial was conducted in this manner changed nothing; the core of it was deadly, terrifyingly serious.

"Bring the prisoner before the court," General Packenham said.

The order was repeated back to the kitchen. "Bring the prisoner before the court," this one and that one shouted, and Alice whispered into my ear, "No, it can't go on this way. It must not, Evan."

"It doesn't matter how it goes on," I said. Then I caught Hunt's eye. He was watching me strangely.

Two militiamen pushed through the crowd, bringing Hans Pohl with them. The boy had been dressed in his filthy, bloodstained uniform—at his own desire, I learned —and his hands were bound behind his back.

"Untie him!" Hunt ordered.

Packenham moved to speak, and then thought better of it. The two militiamen untied the boy's hands, and then he stood stiffly at attention in front of the table. From the moment he had come into the room, Sally had not taken her eyes from him; yet he in turn avoided her eyes and now stared straight ahead of him at General Packenham.

"You stand before a legally constituted military court of this sovereign state," Packenham said. "Do you understand that, sir?"

The boy nodded.

"What is your name?" the General asked.

"Hans Pohl."

"Your regiment?"

"Sixteenth Jager."

"Your rank?"

"Private soldier."

The answers were soft but firm, his accent hardly discernible in the few words he spoke. With his sandy hair and his new freckles from his few days in the sunshine, he might have been one of the lads from the Ridge.

"Read the charge," Packenham said to Crippit, and

the little clerk, his hands shaking with excitement, picked up a long sheet of foolscap, cleared his throat and proceeded to read:

"Military court convened in the township of Ridgefield. Accused, one Hans Pohl, private soldier in the service of the Elector of Hesse and the King of England. The accused, Hans Pohl, private soldier, is charged with murder, premeditated and cruel and wanton. It is charged that on the sixteenth day of May, in the Year of Our Lord, 1781, he was one of a detachment of Hessian soldiers who made an incursion into the territory of the township of Ridgefield. In the course of this incursion, they met with a citizen, one Saul Clamberham, unarmed and dressed in civilian clothes. The said citizen did them no harm and in no way interfered with their progress. Without cause of any kind, they made this civilian, the said Saul Clamberham, prisoner, and without trial or reason, hanged him by the neck until he was dead. The above is alleged by the Court, and the Court intends to prove that the above is the truth and nothing but the whole truth. The Court charges that every member of the detachment of Hessian soldiers was equally guilty of this cruel and wanton murder, and so deserves the punishment in kind. How does the prisoner before the Court plead to this charge?"

The boy appeared not to understand. The courtroom had become very quiet now, and there was no other sound but the breathing of the people packed into it, and then suddenly there was a bustle of movement and voices, and those men in front of the outer door pushed aside to allow Raymond and his son, Jacob, to enter. They stood for a moment in the open space, their eyes unused to the contrast with the brilliant sunshine outside, and then saw us and moved slowly to where we were. Sally rose, giving her father the seat, and sat down cross-legged on the floor. Jacob took his place next to her. Hans Pohl did not turn his head, and the murmur of voices in response to Raymond's entry was stilled by the pounding of Packenham's gavel.

St. August stood up and said to the Hessian, "How do you plead, sir? You must give an answer. Either you are guilty or you are not guilty. Which is it?"

"I don't understand," Hans Pohl said.

"What is there that defies your understanding?" St. August demanded. "The charge was simple and plain. Are you guilty of the murder of one Saul Clamberham or are you not guilty? How do you plead?"

Hans shook his head again.

"Then if you will not plead, I must plead you and accept your silence as a statement of guilt."

"You will not, sir!" I cried out, rising. "This is damnable! The boy speaks kitchen English and no more, and he doesn't understand half the words in that charge."

Packenham was pounding with his gavel now.

"Since when is a man guilty before a trial?" I demanded.

"Who are you, sir?" St. August shouted. "How do you dare interrupt this trial? Who gave you permission to speak?"

"One more word, Feversham," Packenham roared, "and I eject you! You are here by sufferance, sir! Sufferance! One more word and I eject you!"

Hunt rose and stood facing Packenham, who was pounding with his gavel again. The gabble of voices in the background stilled, and Hunt said coldly, his voice hard with restrained anger, "This is a misunderstanding, is it not, Colonel St. August? As I understand it, you were going to plead him not guilty. I think there is nothing else you can do, sir. He has not yet been tried or heard."

"If he pleads guilty, he pleads guilty," St. August insisted. "There is no illegality in that."

"Then make it clear to him."

St. August took a deep breath, held his silence for a moment, and then said, "Hans Pohl, did you murder Saul Clamberham?"

"No," the boy replied. "I don't murder him."

"Then you plead not guilty."

"I don't murder him," the boy repeated.

Hunt was still standing, and now Packenham said, "Will you approach the Court, Squire." Hunt walked to the table, bent over, and Packenham whispered to him. Hunt shook his head. Packenham whispered again, and again Hunt shook his head. Packenham then nodded sourly, and Hunt returned to his seat.

"You may call your first witness," Packenham said to St. August.

The Colonel glanced at Crippit, who ostentatiously riffled through his papers until he found his list of witnesses, and then sang out:

"Call Miss Jenny Perkins!"

"I'm right here, Bosley," Miss Perkins replied, sitting as she was no more than six feet from him.

"Rise and put your hand on the Book."

Miss Perkins went to the table and placed her hand on the Bible.

"Do you swear to tell the truth, the whole truth and nothing but the truth? Say I do."

"I'll say nothing of the sort," Miss Perkins replied. "I am not given to lying. If you don't know that, Bosley Crippit, you're a fool, and I have never taken an oath and I have no intentions of taking one now. It's an unchristian thing."

"This is a different matter, Miss Perkins."

"It is not."

Crippit turned to the General, who was again pounding his gavel to still the laughter. St. August said, "So long as she places her hand on the Book."

"You see that I have," she said.

"Yes. What is your name, madam?"

"I am unmarried, sir. My name is Jenny Perkins. If you had given your attention—"

"Please only answer my questions."

"Very well. Ask sensible questions."

"Did you know one Saul Clamberham?"

"I did."

"How long did you know him?"

"As long as I remember."

"Did you know his family?"

"He had no family. He was a foundling. He was left with Goody Allison by people passing through. Worthless people. They never returned for him. I think he was five years old then. Goody Allison took care of him until she passed on. He was eleven years old then, and after that he just lived hand to mouth and no one took care of him, God forgive us."

"Why do you say God forgive us?" St. August asked curiously.

"Because I am a Christian," she answered matter-of-factly.

Hans Pohl turned his head now to look at her. It was his first movement since he had assumed his position, stone-like, in front of the table; and Miss Perkins appeared to be taken aback. Possibly she had not looked at him before, for the world is full of people and things that we never see or bother to see.

"I am afraid I do not follow you, Miss Perkins," St. August said. He had that sort of a mind. It plodded doggedly.

"If he had proper care or love or home or hearth, sir, he would not have been down on the trail playing his foolish games with the Hessians."

"Do you mean he was irresponsible?"

"He was a halfwit, sir. His mind was addled. He was a small child in a large man's body. He couldn't learn anything, not to read or write even the simplest thing."

"You are the schoolma'am here on the Ridge?"

"I am."

"Did you try to teach Saul Clamberham?"

"Yes, I tried. It was hopeless. He would come to the school, and then he would stay away for months, and then he would come to the school again."

"Why would he come back?"

"Because he wanted so desperately to learn."

"Was he dangerous?"

"Dangerous? How could he be dangerous?" She looked at Hans Pohl now, her glance straight and righteous. She was an intelligent, thoughtful, principled woman, but Hans Pohl was from the outside.

He might look like the sandy-haired boys who lived on the Ridge, but the look served only to disguise the devil that inhabited him. He came from a land that was an inconceivable distance away—five thousand miles, and in all her life Miss Perkins had never been farther than twenty miles from the village of Ridgefield. Until she stood beside him now, she had never seen a German, and for six years she had listened to the terrible barbarisms that were attributed to the Hessians, and had shivered at night, alone in her house, at the creaking of wood, asking herself whether it was not a Hessian come to murder her in her sleep.

"I mean," St. August explained, "did he molest the children or try to hurt people?"

"Saul Clamberham?"

"Yes, Saul Clamberham."

"You should be ashamed of yourself," she informed St. August. "The suggestion is disgusting."

"At the same time, I must ask you."

"He could not hurt a fly." She dabbed at her eyes. "He was gentle."

"Thank you, Miss Perkins. That will do," St. August said.

She went back to her chair and began to weep into her kerchief.

"You may leave the court if you wish, Miss Perkins," General Packenham told her.

She shook her head. She might well be distraught, but she was not going to give up that front seat for anything.

"It's very hot here," General Packenham said, and indeed by now he was perspiring profusely. "Can't we have a window opened? There are delicate women and little children in this room. Must someone faint before we show them a little courtesy?"

There was shuffling and moving to open the windows, and Bosley Crippit called Jacob Heather. Jacob rose and walked up to the table.

"Put your hand on the Book," Crippit told him.

Jacob shook his head.

"Do you understand him, boy? He wants to swear you in for the truth. Put your hand on the Bible and swear to tell the truth."

Again, Jacob shook his head. "We do not swear," he said, his voice a bit shaky. "I must not."

Two of them were too much for Packenham, who declared that the boy damn well would take the oath or he'd know the reason why.

"Let him be, General," Hunt said tiredly, "and let him tell his story. What difference does it make?"

"It must be in the record."

"Well, we won't rightly have a record, because Bosley there cannot get down one word for every three that are spoken. So we might as well let it be and have the boy speak."

St. August sighed in acknowledgment of the strangeness of people who lived on the Ridge, and asked Jacob his name.

"Jacob Heather."

"Well, Jacob, you're a fine-looking lad. How old are you?"

"Twelve years."

"Twelve years indeed. Now will you tell us where you were on the sixteenth of May?"

"I don't know."

"You don't know? How could you possibly not know or remember where you were on the sixteenth of May?"

"Because I don't know when it was," Jacob replied, very conscious of the Hessian boy standing only a few feet away from him.

"Then I must refresh you," St. August said. "It was the day the Hessians hanged Saul Clamberham."

Jacob looked at Hans now. Hans did not move, and like a shadow woe crept over the small boy's face.

"Do you remember the day?"

Jacob nodded.

"You must speak up and answer yes or no."

"Yes," Jacob whispered.

"Where were you then, when you saw the Hessians?"

"On Hightop."

"I presume that Hightop is a hill. What were you doing there?"

"Hiding," Jacob said.

"Why weren't you at school?"

"It was a meditation day."

"What do you mean, a meditation day?"

"Thee remain at home and look into thy heart."

"But you were at Hightop?"

Packenham hammered with his gavel to still the laughter.

"Yes, sir."

"And what did you see there?"

"The Hessians."

"Why didn't you run away when you saw them?"

"I was too frightened."

"Was Saul Clamberham with the Hessians?"

"Yes—yes, sir." He looked at Hans again.

"What were they doing to him?"

Jacob shook his head.

"Then why didn't he run away?"

"They had a rope around his neck and his hands were tied."

"Come now, Jacob, don't be afraid. No Hessian can hurt you here. Tell us what they did to Saul Clamberham."

"They threw—they threw—" He did not actually begin to cry, but his face was tight with agony; and he turned then to look at his sister, Sally, but she was staring down at her hands in her lap.

Alice asked me, "Must they do this to him?"

"Only he saw it."

"Everyone knows what he saw."

"Everyone wants to hear it again," I murmured. "Death is very special. See how everyone listens."

Everyone listened. It was so still in that room that the buzzing of flies against the windowpanes sounded as loud as the rasp of a wood saw.

"Come now, Jacob. Be a man. Speak up."

Slowly, Jacob said, "They threw the rope over a tree and pulled him up into the tree."

"Who did they pull up into the tree?"

"Saul Clamberham!" Jacob cried desperately.

"Fine lad. Now how did they do it?"

"With the rope."

"Yes, I know that they hanged him with the rope. But Saul Clamberham was a large man. Did one Hessian pull him up into the tree?"

Jacob stood silent.

"Come, Jacob. You must answer my question. Otherwise, how can we know the truth? Now, how many men pulled the rope and hanged Saul Clamberham?"

Still Jacob remained silent.

"Was it one man? Two men? Answer, boy!"

"Why do you torture him?" my wife burst out.

Packenham pounded his gavel. "I will not have interruptions, madam! That is plain!"

"Three men, four men? Five men? Or was it the whole detachment on the rope?" St. August loomed over the boy. "How many? How many? Answer!"

"I don't remember," Jacob pleaded.

"Then think! Or is it that you don't want to remember?"

"I don't remember."

"Didn't you tell Squire Hunt that there were sixteen men and a drummer, and another man on a horse?"

"I don't know—I don't remember."

"But you told that to Squire Hunt?"

"Yes," Jacob admitted.

"How did you know?"

"I don't remember."

"But you knew then. You told Squire Hunt that there were sixteen Hessians and the drummer. How did you know that then?"

"I counted them."

"All of them?"

"Yes."

"And you were right!" St. August cried, a note of triumph in his voice. "Good lad! Cool lad! Someday you'll make a fine soldier, you will, yes indeed. There were sixteen Hessian foot and a drummer—right on the nose. Yes, you were frightened. Who wouldn't be, with those Hessians right there, ready to hang you as high as poor Saul Clamberham? But not too frightened that you didn't keep your head and count them, so that you could give Squire Hunt the precise information he needed to mount his attack on these contemptible creatures. Now let me ask you this, Jacob, do you refuse to answer now because every last one of those men put their hands on the rope and dragged Saul Clamberham to his death? Is that it?"

"No," Jacob burst out. "There were four men."

"Ah, now you know there were four men. Possibly there were six men? Or ten men?"

"No."

"You are sure? Will you swear to that?"

Jacob shook his head miserably. He was crying now.

"Let the boy be," Hunt said. "Be damned with the number! What does it matter how many men pulled the rope? The detachment hanged him."

"I think it matters," St. August said. "I think it matters very much indeed, sir. I think that this man"—pointing to Hans Pohl—"pulled the rope with the others, and I intend to have the truth."

"Then get it from someone else and let the boy be."

"That's up to the Court, sir." He turned to Packenham, who after a moment or two nodded and said:

"Let the boy sit down."

Jacob ran to Sally and plopped down in front of her, his head in her lap. Crippit picked up his list and called Raymond Heather. As Raymond rose, Crippit said to Packenham, "Shall I try to swear him, your Excellency?"

"He's the boy's father. Be damned with it!"

"State your name," St. August said.

"Raymond Heather."

"Are you the father of Jacob Heather, the boy who just testified?"

"Yes."

"Did he tell you what he saw when the Hessians hanged Saul Clamberham?"

"Yes, he told me."

"Did he tell you how many men were on the rope?"

"Yes. He told me that four men dragged the rope, God forgive them and rest their souls."

"We are not asking for your preachments, sir. We ask for the truth."

"I gave thee the truth."

"And what would it have been if your son had not spoken of four men?"

"Still it would have been four men. That was what he told me. The boy doesn't lie."

"And I suppose you do not lie?" St. August said. And when Raymond did not respond, he demanded, "Does this religion of yours forbid you to lie, or does it give you license to lie when the mood takes you to lie?"

"It forbids me to lie," Raymond answered, "for when I lie there is no refuge for me or place to conceal it."

"You gave this Hessian, Hans Pohl, shelter in your house, did you not?"

"I sheltered him. He was sick and wounded. I could not turn him away. I was forbidden to turn him away."

"Who forbade you?"

"My faith."

"So this faith of yours forbids you to lie and it forbids you to turn away an enemy soldier. Then why did you lie about the Hessian you sheltered?"

Again, Raymond was silent.

"Is it no lie to conceal what you knew your neighbors sought? You live in peace and safety because we take up arms to fight and die, and yet when a word would mean safety and security to those who protect you—you chose to be silent. If that is no lie, then I don't know what falsehood is."

"I chose between a man's life and a lie. Thus I lied," Raymond admitted.

"Yet you ask us to believe that you are not lying now, when you tell us that your son spoke the truth? When the father's a liar, you ask us to believe that the son spoke truthfully?"

Sitting where she was, her brother's head buried in her skirts, Sally said quietly, "It's enough. It's enough, please."

Raymond looked at St. August, and St. August knew enough about a victory not to press it.

"You may go back to your seat, sir," he said.

Hunt was the next witness. He stood somberly next

to the Hessian boy, his great bulk making the Hessian
appear smaller than he was.

"You were here at this inn when Jacob Heather came
with the word about the Hessians?"

"Yes, sir."

"Did he tell you how many Hessians there were?"

"Yes, he did. Sixteen Hessians and the drummer and
the officer. His count was right."

"Did he tell you how many dragged the rope that
hanged Saul Clamberham?"

"No."

"Why not?"

"Because I didn't ask him."

"Were you not curious, Squire Hunt?"

"Not at that moment, no, Colonel. At that moment, I
had only one thought—that the Hessians must be
stopped."

"And what did you do then?"

"I rode to Hightop with Doctor Feversham. I hoped
that they might have done their work poorly and that
Saul was alive."

"But he was dead."

"Yes, sir, he was dead."

"And there was no indication of how many men were
on the rope that had hanged him?"

"No, sir."

"Would you guess?"

"I would not. It makes no difference who held the
rope. The Hessians hanged him."

"I agree with you, Squire. The Hessians hanged him."

Then Salem Alan told the story of how his dog, Duklik, had dug up the uniform, and then I was called.

"You saw no need to inform Squire Hunt as to the
whereabouts of the Hessian, Doctor Feversham?"

"I am a physician, not an informer."

"A physician to our enemy?"

"A physician to anyone who is sick."

"As I understand it, you held the rank of colonel in our army?"

"I still hold the title, Colonel St. August."

"Perhaps—perhaps not for long, sir. And did you know how many men were on the drag rope?"

"Yes."

"How many?"

"Four."

"And where did your knowledge of this come from, Doctor Feversham?"

"From Jacob Heather, who was the only witness to the hanging."

"No, sir," St. August said, unable to resist the slightest smirk. "Not at all. There was another witness."

"Who?" I could not help asking.

"The Hessian, Hans Pohl. As for you, Doctor, I am quite finished with you."

All through this, Hans Pohl had been standing stiffly in front of the table. I marveled at his control and his will.

"You do not have to testify if you do not wish to," St. August said to the boy. "We are not British. We have no Star Chamber proceedings. We do not force men to testify against their will. But if you want to speak and answer my questions, we will be glad to listen to you."

"I will answer questions. I do not murder anyone."

"I did not ask you that. You will answer only when a question is asked of you."

The boy nodded. Sally was watching him now. Jacob sat on the floor, staring at his hands, full of an agony he neither understood nor could cope with, an outsider in the only world he ever knew, imprisoned in that total helplessness that only a child experiences.

"Where did your detachment come from?"

"From New York."

"How did you come to Connecticut?"

"On British frigate."

"What was the military purpose of the voyage?" And when Hans hesitated, St. August said, "If you don't understand my questions, say so. Your English appears to be good enough. Where did you learn to speak English?"

"I am three years in America."

"I see. Now you say that you came from the British frigate that sailed into Long Island Sound. I ask you, what was the military purpose of the warship?"

"I do not know."

"Why was your detachment landed and sent up to the Ridge?"

"I do not know that. Such things are not for me."

"Yet soldiers talk, officers talk. You would have heard something."

"No."

"How did they come to take Saul Clamberham prisoner?"

"He follow us—maybe a mile. We see him in woods. He try to hide, but not so good, no? We all talk about Yankee man who is following us, and sergeant ask captain what to do? Captain Hauser say pace one-half mile, one thousand pace, and then take him. Sergeant tell off six men and tell them when signal is called, they go into woods and take the Yankee man. Then they take him."

"Did Saul Clamberham fight back? Did he resist?"

"No."

"What did you do then?"

"We stand at ease and wait for captain's decision."

"And what was his decision?"

"He say the Yankee man is spy."

"Why? What evidence did he have?"

"This man, Clamberham, he has piece of—" He groped for the word. "From schoolhouse, you write with chalk. Slate. On slate are marks, one for each man. So is information, and captain tells him he is making intelligence and only spies make intelligence."

"Did Clamberham know what the captain said? Did Captain Hauser speak in German or in English?"

"Captain Hauser is here only—five month. He knows no English. My father—"

"Your father? What has your father got to do with this?"

"My father is sergeant," the boy said, his voice breaking. "My father speak English, but not good."

St. August paused. I felt my wife's hand gripping my wrist.

"My father told the Yankee man."

"And then?"

"He did not want to die," the boy said woefully.

"No, he did not want to die," St. August repeated. "He certainly did not want to die."

Packenham broke in at this point. "You heard the testimony here to the effect that this man, Saul Clamberham, was a halfwit. Do you feel proud because you hanged a halfwit?"

Hans Pohl shook his head.

"Speak up!"

"We don't know he is halfwit."

"Were there numbers on the slate?" St. August demanded.

"Marks."

"And it did not strike you as strange that a grown man could not write numbers?"

"Even some men in my regiment—they cannot write down numbers, no? They don't read or write."

"But you—you, yourself, Hans Pohl, did you see nothing strange in the foolish behavior of this man, Clamberham?"

"I see something strange, yes."

"And it occurred to you that he might have been a halfwit?"

"I think he is a little crazy, yes."

"But you did nothing?"

"What could I do?" Hans Pohl asked. "If I talk to Captain Hauser, I am punished."

"You could talk to your father."

The boy shook his head again.

"Then you did nothing. You stood by while this unspeakable murder took place, and you raised no hand to stop it."

The boy remained still, stiff as a ramrod, silent.

"How was he hanged?" St. August asked harshly.

"The rope—over the tree," haltingly.

"And how many men dragged the rope and played the role of hangman?"

"Four."

"Who were those four? Can you name them?"

"Private Schwartz, Private Messerbaum, Private Schimmel—I think, I am not sure."

"And the fourth?"

"I don't remember."

"Was it you?"

"No!" he cried.

"Are you a Christian?" St. August demanded.

"Yes."

"Then you understand what it means to take an oath, to put your immortal soul in jeopardy?"

"Yes, I understand."

"And you still maintain that you did not act as hangman?"

"No, I am not hangman."

"Then let us suppose your Captain Hauser had ordered you to act as hangman—what would you have done?"

"I am good soldier," the boy replied woefully. "I obey orders."

11

The Verdict

THE COURT HAD ADJOURNED for three hours, until four o'clock in the afternoon, at which time, General Packenham had announced, he would deliver the verdict. I had sent Alice home in the buggy, for she felt she could bear no more of it, and I asked her to have Rodney Stephan bring a saddled horse to the inn that evening.

The crowd had emptied out of the inn and had gone off to work or home or food or to wherever their need was, for while the verdict was still to come, no one had any question as to what it might be. I was stopped by three or four people who had various and sundry ailments, taking advantage of their visit to town coinciding with mine, and then I made my way down the street to where Raymond had hitched his wagon. He saw me coming and waited, or possibly he had been waiting until now for me to leave the front of the inn. Sally and Jacob sat in the wagon, their backs straight, their faces set, aware that they were the focus for every pair of eyes in the crowd and enduring it as best they could. Ebenezer Calvil, who was mostly drunk and always foul-mouthed, stood a few feet from the wagon, swaying back and forth, and as I came there, he was saying:

"—not young, sissy, but on four sides I be a better man than any Hessian"—he turned to me, grinning, large, dirty, the purple veins standing out on his nose and cheeks—"which the doctor here will bear out, him being a sort of specialist on Hessians."

Raymond was staring at him with the uneasy patience of a man incapable of violence or threat.

"Think I got a future with the lassie, Doc?"

"You don't have much of a future with anything," I told him coldly, "and if you don't stop drinking, you'll be dead before the year's out. Now get out of here."

He shook his head and stared at me. "Who in hell do you think you're talking to, you lousy lobster?"

"Get out of here!"

Sally never moved or looked at him, but her lips were trembling. Jacob began to cry again, holding himself as still as his sister, fighting the tears that rolled down his cheeks.

"She wanted to stay," Raymond explained, "but it's no use to stay, is it?"

"No, I don't think so."

Ebenezer Calvil still stood there, holding his ground. Now he spat on the wagon.

"Will thee come to us and tell us?"

"Yes, I'll come."

Raymond climbed into the wagon and drove off, Calvil flinging curses after him, and I walked back to the inn. I went into the taproom where I had left my hat. The candles had burned down, and in the semidarkness I thought at first that it was deserted, and then I noticed Hunt sitting at one side of the room.

I would have passed through without speaking to him, for I had thought that I would go to Packenham again with some sort of plea or bluff, and surely I had nothing to say to Hunt, but he called to me, and I walked over to him. He was sprawled in his chair, his booted legs thrust out, his coat off and his waistcoat and shirt open.

"What can I do for you?" I asked him.

"Did the Heathers go home?"

"Yes."

"That's the best thing they could have done. I didn't want them here when the verdict is said."

"I imagine you didn't."

"You're an unforgiving bastard, Feversham. Well, so am I. How did the girl take it?"

"How would you expect?"

"Damn it, I've been fair. Don't make me out to be some kind of inhuman swine."

"Is that what you wanted to say to me?"

"Damn you, Feversham, I've been fair. Give me a nod for that. I could have made life hell for those people. In your eyes, they've done nothing. In my eyes and in the eyes of most people around here, they've betrayed our cause."

"I never said they did nothing."

"Are you pulling out of it now, Feversham?"

"Not truly. In my eyes, they performed an act of human kindness."

"You amaze me, Feversham."

"Still, you could have made life hell for them."

"You give the devil his due, don't you?"

"What damn difference does it make what I think?"

"None." A long pause, Hunt watching me in the gloom, and then he asked, "Was that Calvil yelling out there?"

"Yes."

"I'll remember that. I'll break that bastard's back."

"Accolade. Defender of womanhood," I said with approval.

"Don't go out of your way to be nasty, Feversham. It comes naturally. I suppose you're off to plead with Packenham now."

"Do you object?"

"No. Go ahead, for all the difference it will make with that pompous son of a bitch. Personally, I think he hates your guts, and after what you said to him, I don't blame him. What happened at Saratoga?"

"What happens at any battle. He lost his nerve and decided to run away."

"Did he?"

"No. Stark caught him and beat him half to death."

"With his hands?"

"With the flat of his sword. Have you ever seen a man whipped with a sword?"

"And you're going to ask him for favors?" Hunt smiled and shook his head. "Go ahead, Feversham, go ahead."

"Where is he?"

"Upstairs, in the big double room. He's having a bite of dinner with the charming St. August. One works hard to keep a paunch like that."

"I admire the company you keep," I said as I walked toward the door, and he snapped at me:

"Feversham!"

I paused.

"I do what I must do, Feversham. I don't give two

damns what else you think of me, but I want to make that plain. I do what I must do."

"As we all do, Squire."

Upstairs, I knocked, and St. August sang out cheerfully, "Come in, come in!"

They sat at the table in their shirtsleeves, and on the table was a platter with two roast ducks and a great apple pastry. They were eating with a determination that precluded their taking their eyes off the food, tearing pieces out of the ducks and licking the fat from their fingers and spooning eagerly from the depths of the pastry. It was a long moment or two before they turned to examine their visitor, and then their bright faces darkened.

"I don't think we have anything to say to you, Feversham," the General told me. He took a large spoonful of apples, and said to St. August, "Dried apples."

"It's June," St. August apologized.

"Better than nothing, I suppose. What do you want, Feversham?"

"I want to plead."

"Nonsense," Packenham said, sputtering through a mouthful of duck. "Men like you don't plead. Trouble with your kind, Feversham, is that you take everyone else for a fool. Take it for granted that everyone is transparent but no one sees through you. The duck is gamy," he said to St. August.

"Wild duck?"

"Too fat. Not wild duck at all. It's the slop they feed them. They feed them old fish. Go ahead and plead, Feversham."

"Don't hang the boy. I ask you that with all my heart, General Packenham. I beg you, don't hang him. Sell him out as a chattel. That's punishment enough."

"For murder? Come, come, Feversham."

"No, no—he's no more guilty of murder than I am."

"Indeed?"

"Please—I beg it of you, as an officer and a gentleman."

"I return the compliment, Feversham, although damned if I know how an officer and a gentleman survives up here on this lousy Ridge. The food is not fit for pigs, and the beer's warm as piss and sour too. What do they have for a sweet, Colonel?"

St. August raised the cover of a crockery dish. "Honey and clotted cream."

"Cream sweet?"

St. August dipped his finger into the dish and licked it. "Sweet as the honey."

"Now they've turned the trick. Have a beer with us, Feversham, and let bygones be bygones. Pleading doesn't become you. You heard the evidence, did you not?"

I closed the door behind me and went downstairs. The kitchen of the inn was packed with men, the smell of food, the stink of beer, and the hubbub of voices. The arguments raged hot and heavy, only a few taking the side of the Hessian, and those more for the pleasure of the dispute than out of any conviction of his innocence. I went through to the courtroom, where Hunt still sprawled on his chair, and he raised an arm to salute me, and asked:

"Did you soften the General's heart, Feversham?"

"He would listen to you."

"Let the Hessian hang, Feversham. You're a stranger here anyway, no matter how you cut it. America is strange to you, and the Ridge is even stranger. There is nothing about us you will ever really know, because we are like nothing else you ever encountered, and if you think we are Englishmen two or three or four genera-

tions removed, you are making a great mistake. You ask
for mercy—but do you think we took this continent
and made it ours with mercy? Like hell we did! We paid
with blood every inch of the way. My grandmother had
eleven children, and two of them survived. There was a
winter when they ate grass roots they dug up from the
frozen ground. These fields are as fat and green as a
sow's ass, but find another people anywhere who put up
a thousand miles of stone wall, every lousy stone dug
out of those same fields, and all of it in two generations.
We built these houses and cleared these fields with our
own hands, and we fought the Indians because what was
ours had to be ours, and what was right was the thing
we did to live here in this damned wilderness, and now
we've fought the British six years, and we'll fight them
six more years or sixty years if we have to. So I can't
explain to you what happened inside of me when I saw
Saul Clamberham's body hanging there."

"You didn't give two damns for Saul Clamberham,"
I said.

"You're right, not two damns. I had no sleepless hours
over him. But I will tell you what I gave two damns
about—the Hessians. When they marched up here onto
the Ridge, my stomach turned as sour as bad wine.
There's a difference between us, Feversham. I know how
to hate, and you don't, and hate is a lovely thing. A
man is strong with hate, stronger than you imagine. Do
you think I knew what the outcome would be when I
took those men down there to Buskin's place? I did not.
These are no soldiers, these militia here on the Ridge.
They faced one battle in their whole lives, and then
when the shooting started, most of them ran away, and
they were so frightened of Hessians that they shook at

the thought of them. You saw them when they came down there to Buskin's. How many of them imagined that they would live through the day? And you want me to mourn the Hessians? No, sir. You fail to understand me."

"Yes, I fail to understand you, Squire Hunt," I admitted.

"Then let it be at that, and plead no more, Feversham."

I was thinking, "I plead only for myself." But it was no use to say that to him. He was right. My skill at hatred was poor indeed, and in some ways, Abraham Hunt knew me better than I knew myself.

Now people were beginning to drift back into the room, but not as many as before. These were not a people to give a whole day in the spring to the life of one Hessian. There was seed to be planted and grass to be cut and stock to feed and fences to mend, so no more than a few dozen men had taken their place in the room when Oscar Latham lit new candles, and when General Packenham and Colonel St. August and Clerk Crippit took their seats behind the table. General Packenham, the buttons on his waistcoat open to accommodate duck and pastry and beer, pounded with his gavel, and Crippit rose and read from his foolscap:

"This military court of the Commonwealth of Connecticut is now in session, General Jonah Packenham presiding." He put the paper down then and looked at the General.

"Have them stand."

"Everybody rise," Crippit called out.

We stood up.

"Bring in the Hessian," Packenham said.

He was already entering the room, the two militiamen on either side of him. He stood at attention in front of the table.

"Do you have anything to say, Hans Pohl, before this Court passes sentence upon you?"

It was difficult for the boy to speak. His voice broke and thickened with emotion as he forced the words out. "I do not murder any man. But I am a Hessian soldier. I am a Jager. If I must die, I will die like a Jager."

He must have rehearsed the few words over and over.

"Then hear the sentence of this Court. You have been found guilty of premeditated murder of an American citizen. We have heard all the evidence given and we have pondered upon it, and we find no extenuating circumstances. Therefore, we sentence you to be hanged by the neck until dead, and may God have mercy on your soul."

Packenham covered his mouth to muffle the sound of his belching. The boy fought to maintain his dignity, but he was only a boy, and the tears rolled down his cheeks.

12

The Gallows

THERE WAS STILL AN HOUR of daylight left when I finally
returned home that day, and when Rodney Stephan had
taken my horse, I was so tired I could barely walk. Alice
was in the garden, tying the grapevine into place over
the arbor frame that Rodney Stephan had built. It was
two weeks since we had bothered with it. We were both
of us fascinated with the project of growing the kind of
long, living arbor that was such a favorite in England
but which I had never seen on the Ridge, and we had
begun two years before by encouraging two wild vines
that happened to be growing in the proper place. The
grapes were small, purple and sour and apparently
native to that part of Connecticut; although I am not
sure that any grapes were to be found in New England
before the white men came, in spite of the story that
Vikings had once found this place and called it Vineland.
The grapes were not fit to eat and made a very poor sort
of wine, but the leaves were wide and beautiful, and
already the arbor was a pleasant place to sit.

I sat on our bench and stretched my legs gratefully. It was a warm, kind June evening, with only a gentle breeze to move the air. Alice went on working, watching me, and then she asked me about the Heathers.

"Did they take it badly?"

"I'm afraid so."

"And Sally?"

"I don't know," I said. "The verdict was no surprise to her. They were there, as you know, and then they left. She appears to have walled herself off—but then I don't know those people. I thought I did, but I don't."

"Rodney Stephan says Packenham and St. August never even discussed the verdict. He says they sat in their rooms at the inn and stuffed themselves with food."

"There's very little Rodney Stephan misses, isn't there? Did he also tell you that I saw them?"

"That you pleaded with them and then had a bitter argument with Abraham Hunt."

"Not bitter and hardly any argument at all."

She looked at me strangely then, as if I had betrayed something.

"He is what he is." I shrugged.

She put aside her work on the vine and sat down beside me, placing her hand over mine. "Don't be angry with me, Evan."

"Why should I be?"

"Because whatever I say, it's because I am so full of death and so sick of it."

"I'm damned if I know what that means."

"Perhaps I don't know myself. When you told Sally Heather that it was a death sentence, did she weep?"

"No."

"Then what did she do?"

"She went to her father and embraced him," I answered, thinking of how that alien, curious family of Quakers were, all of them there in the kitchen and knit together with something that I did not know but yearned for so desperately that my whole body ached.

"Evan?" Alice said.

"Yes."

"Please tell me this. If you had known Sarah Heather eighteen years ago, before she was married, would you have asked her to marry you?"

"Alice, I was not even in America eighteen years ago."

"But if you had been?"

"That's a damn foolish question, isn't it?"

"Please—try to answer me."

"Then the answer is no. I would not have married her."

"Why?"

"Because it's not enough to share love. There's agony to be shared, and I don't think she could ever sense what my agony is, they are all of them so far from it and so removed from it."

"As I am not?"

"As you are not."

She was crying now, and I said to her, "Come to bed, and we'll hold each other for a while."

"And cling to nothing?"

"Nothing or something, I no longer know."

That was a Saturday, and the next morning, Alice went off to church. I have no surgery on Sunday, so I put on old clothes and went to work with Rodney Stephan in the garden. When we work together, his conversation is mostly of horses, for he knows horses well and knows of my own love for them; but today his conversation took another turn, and he wondered whether in church they would tell their God about the trial and the verdict.

"I presume God is aware of it."

"So be it, Doctor, but should he not be told?"

"Have you never been baptized?"

"Nay, nay, Doctor," he answered in that curious way of speaking that he has, "for they slew the old people, and the Christian God would not welcome me."

"But that was a long time ago."

"In Christian time, yes, but in the great time it is today, and my people lived with the great time."

I let that go by, since I knew that it would be fruitless to ask him to explain what he meant. We were setting out seedlings for Indian beans, and for a while we worked on in silence, and then I asked him why he thought God should be told. He turned his wrinkled, leathery face to me, squinted thoughtfully for a moment or two, and then said:

"Forgive me asking, but ye be no Christian, Doctor?"

"What on earth gave you that idea?"

" 'Tis Sundays gave me the notion."

That was reasonable, and I asked him what his point was.

"Ye see," he said, "it's hard for a Christian to understand. I be a fair hunter, so if I draw me a bead on a deer, I beseech him first and tell him the circumstances. With the old people, the deer was like God is with the Christians, but different."

"What on earth do you mean?"

He shook his head. He was always baffled when he said something of this sort and I asked him what he meant, and I imagine there was no language at his command that could put what he meant into words.

"What circumstances do you tell the deer?"

"The deer is hungry, but I be in greater appetite. If the deer lives, I die. Then the deer must die and I will live, and this the deer knows."

"How does the deer know it?"

"I tell him." He thought for a moment and then added, "He will never be angered at me."

"Suppose he were angered," I said impatiently, for I was annoyed at his nonsense, "what could a dead deer do to you?"

"I would be full of sickness, and I would lay me down and die."

"What damn nonsense!" I exclaimed. "What the devil can a deer do to make you sick?"

"The deer be me and I be the deer," he said gravely.

"You are full of wretched superstition, Rodney Stephan, and I am amazed that all the years you worked here made so small an impression on you."

At lunch, Alice told me about the sermon. Dorset had taken for his text, "Judge not, lest ye be judged."

"It was a very good sermon," she said. "It was a civilized sermon. I wish you had heard it, Evan."

"You are an incredible people," I told her. "I think you are the most incredible people that ever appeared on this earth. Do you know that they will hang the Hessian tomorrow?"

"Then is it wrong for me to sit in church and weep inside of myself?"

"I am not talking about what is right and what is wrong, Alice. God Almighty, if ever there was a man who did not know what is right or wrong, you are looking at him now."

"I have heard," she said, "that in your country they will hang a man for stealing a purse."

"Yes," I agreed, "or for stealing a crust of bread. There are three hundred and eighty-two offenses in England for which a man may be hanged, but it's not my country. Will you never understand that this is my country, that this wretched, rocky ridge of land here in Connecticut is the only place I ever loved, the only place that ever gave me a moment or two of peace or happiness?"

She remained silent for a little while, and then she asked me, "Will you have surgery tomorrow?"

"No."

"What shall I tell the people who come?"

"Tell them that it's a day of penance and that Doctor Feversham has gone to see a man hanged."

"No. Why will you go?"

"Because I must."

"I would not want to see it."

"I don't want to see it, but I must."

I awakened in the early dawn, before the sun rose, and took my clothes and crept silently down to the surgery, where I dressed myself, and then I went into the kitchen and took some water but could not bear the thought of food on my sour stomach. When I came to the barn, Rodney Stephan was already there, and the sun was just tipping the hills, dropping its lovely pink warmth into the mist-filled bottoms. The crows began to call and awakened the roosters, and suddenly the first rays of the new sun touched us. We stood for a few minutes without a word being said, and then Rodney Stephan asked me what horse I desired.

"Give me the bay."

She was a gentle, intelligent beast, alive to the slightest desire on my part, and when I sat in the saddle, she moved out and toward the town as if she knew what was in my mind. I let her walk at her own easy pace, and she moved me in a dreamlike way through the mist and past the endless stone walls that lined the road.

When I reached town, the Benton brothers, who were the best carpenters in Ridgefield, were already at work on the gallows, the drumbeat of their hammers filling the air. They had already framed out a platform about five feet high in the middle of the Common, and now, with help from the boys who had paused to watch on their way to school, they were raising the gallows post, sliding it into the hole they had dug to receive it. They would then tie it into the platform, frame an opening under it, and the gallows would be done.

I dismounted and stood watching for a while, and presently I noticed that Abraham Hunt stood beside me.

"Good morning," he said.

I nodded. Then a time of silence, and then he said, not unkindly, "Will the Heathers claim the body?"

"I don't know."

"Will you ask them, Feversham?"

"I'll ask them."

Then I mounted and rode down the street to the Congregational church, and tied my horse and went to the parsonage, which was next to the church. Ziporah Dorset opened the door for me, and then stared at me in bewildered embarrassment. Poor woman, she was caught in the center of it, and suddenly her eyes filled with tears and I had a sense of my own cruelty in never looking at her or knowing her as a human being, or what she felt and suffered.

"John is in his study, Doctor Feversham," she whispered. "I'll tell him you are here." She clasped and unclasped her hands nervously. "Will you sit down, please?"

Her husband must have heard our voices, for he opened the door to his room and came into the parlor. He was in his shirtsleeves, and he begged my pardon.

"Come in, please, Doctor Feversham," he said.

I followed him into the little room he called his study, the walls full of books, the rug threadbare, the few pieces of pine furniture worn and rickety, myself wondering whether anyone in these colonies was quite as poor as a Congregational minister on the Ridge. He motioned me to a seat, and then sat himself down behind the old table he used as a desk and stared at me, attempting, I am sure, to think of something he might say that would have meaning for me.

I told him of my few words with Hunt. "You will allow him to be buried in the churchyard with the Hessians?"

"Oh, of course, of course."

"Did you mark the Hessian graves?"

"We will. I must go to Danbury and talk to the stonecutters. I have not had the opportunity yet. You know, we are not a wealthy church, Doctor Feversham. You know, we have the names of the men, and I thought of a stone with all the names inscribed upon it. That's all the memory that will ever be of them. But the truth is—" He shook his head. "We just don't have the money."

"How much will it cost?"

"A hundred dollars Spanish or ten pounds sterling. It would have to be a large stone."

I took two five-guinea goldpieces out of my pocket and laid them on the table.

"Add the boy's name to it, please."

"Of course." Then he said uneasily, "Should I have some small service here at the church?"

"I am going to ask Raymond Heather what to do. Do the Quakers have any special ritual for the dead? I'm afraid I don't know."

"They're good Christians," Dorset said miserably. "If they want to, it might be better that they should do it. It's not easy for me to say this, Doctor Feversham, but it might be better."

"You will have the grave dug?"

"Yes. Oh, yes, indeed."

I rose to go, and Dorset walked with me to the door. "Doctor Feversham," he said, "don't judge us too harshly. You have been a soldier, and you know how merciless war is."

"Is war merciless?" I asked him. "Or are men merciless?"

"I can only say, God forgive us. What else can I say?"

I rode out to Raymond Heather's place then, but slowly, allowing the bay to walk the distance; for I was not eager to come there, and there was much that I had to think about. It was midday when I reached the farm. Sarah opened the door for me. They had just finished their meal, or what small part of it they were able to eat, and I stood with Sarah, while Raymond bent his head and offered their silent thanksgiving for their bread. When Sally raised her head, she said:

"It's good to see thee, Evan." Her face was wan and drawn, but her voice was calm.

"Have thee had food, Evan?" Sarah asked me.

"I am not hungry."

Jacob got up suddenly and bolted from the house.

"Sit here," Sarah said, giving me his chair. She put

bread in front of me, and cheese and butter, and poured me a mixture of warm coffee and milk. Sarah and Sally cleared the table while I ate, and Raymond sat watching me in silence. Then Sally took Joanna in her lap and sat down by the hearth.

I finished eating, and then said to Raymond, "I must talk about some painful things. Shall we be by ourselves?"

"Evan," Sally said quietly, "if thee will talk about Hans Pohl, I would hear what you have to say."

"All right. I spoke to the Squire this morning, and he asked me whether you would want to claim the body. I said I would speak to you."

"I thought of that," Raymond said. "If they will allow it, we would take the body to our meetinghouse."

"They will. I also spoke to Pastor Dorset. He will have a grave dug where the other Hessians are buried in his churchyard."

"I considered that we might bury him in our own place."

"No," Sally said. "Let him lie with his father. That's the way he would want it."

"As you will," Raymond agreed.

"Where should he lie until he is buried?" I asked.

"In our meetinghouse."

"Then I'll ride back and tell Rodney Stephan to bring our wagon into Ridgefield."

"We'll take him in my wagon," Raymond said. "Sally will go with me, and the two of us will be there when the thing is done."

"No," I said. "No. I have seen such things. It's not a thing that a child should see."

"Evan," Sally said, "must I always remind thee that I am not a child?"

"Let her go, Evan," Sarah said. "We don't turn our eyes away from the world. We accept it as it is. Otherwise, even our own faith will not save us."

"What has faith got to do with this murderous act?"

"More than thee might imagine. Please, Evan, don't reason with us today."

"And I must see Hans before he dies," Sally said.

"Thee must make it possible," Raymond said. "This is not of the moment. We have talked a great deal about these things, and thee must not take our wishes lightly."

"All right," I sighed, and stood up. "Let's harness your horses now, Raymond." I looked at my watch. "There are only about three hours remaining."

I rode behind the wagon into the town. We tied the horses at the church, and then the three of us walked to the inn, where the Hessian was being held. Already people were drifting toward the gallows place for the hanging, and in the big kitchen of the inn, Hunt and Packenham and St. August and a half-dozen militiamen were waiting, drinking beer or munching bread and cheese. When I appeared, a sudden silence fell. I nodded at Hunt.

"A word with you, Squire?"

I stepped into the pantry, and he followed me there.

"I have Raymond Heather and his daughter outside."

"Now that was a damn fool thing to do, to bring them here!"

"It was not my doing. She has a will of her own."

"Well, if they're here, they're here."

"She wants to see the Hessian."

"Be damned, Feversham! What kind of nonsense is that? What good will it do for them to see each other now?"

"No good as far as you and I are concerned. But it is

something she wants and she wants it desperately. As far as I can see, it's the most important thing in the world to her right now."

"Tell her no."

"Hunt, I can't tell her no."

"Feversham, don't you understand that Packenham's running this now? I am out of it."

"I don't think you're out of it, Squire."

"I know what Packenham will say."

"I don't think you give a damn what Packenham will say. I think you despise him as much as I do. You did this thing, not Packenham. Are you going to tell me that you haven't enough guts to stand up to it?"

I thought he was going to explode at me, but he held onto himself, and then stood and stared at me, breathing deeply.

"Do it, Hunt. Do this one thing."

He took a deep breath and said, "Bring her around to the taproom. I don't want her coming through the kitchen."

I went outside then and told Raymond to wait for us. Then I took Sally into the taproom. It was still empty, as if some pall hung over it that could not be dissipated. Latham, the innkeeper, had put the chairs and tables back into their old places, but evidently he could not bring himself to open the place for custom yet—or else custom avoided it until the curse ebbed out of it. We waited there for a few minutes, and then Hunt appeared from the kitchen and said brusquely:

"Follow me."

He took us through the serving stairs to the second floor, where two militiamen stood in front of a door.

"Open it," Hunt said.

They opened the door, to reveal the boy, lying on his back on a low trundle bed. The room was one of those tiny cubbyholes under the eaves that Latham rented out to travelers. The boy did not move.

"Hans," Sally said softly.

He raised up and swung around, amazement and despair on his face, and Sally went into the room. Then the boy stood up, facing her.

"Fifteen minutes," Hunt said.

I closed the door. The militiamen stood uneasily, grinning foolishly until Hunt told them that he saw nothing amusing for two idiots to grin at. From behind the door, the low sound of voices, but no words that I could distinguish, and Hunt took a fat turnip watch out of his waistcoat and stared at it.

"Fifteen minutes, twenty minutes—what difference does it make?" I asked him.

"Don't push me too far, Feversham."

A beam of sunlight came into the narrow hallway from a single half-moon window, and I watched the dust motes dance and whirl. The militiamen shifted and shuffled their feet and cleared their throats. And the minutes passed, and I thought of what Rodney Stephan had said about the great time, where there is no past and no future either.

Then Sally opened the door. The Hessian boy stood with his back to her, nor did he turn around when she left the room, and I guessed that he had been crying and could not bear for us in the hallway to see his tears.

I took her downstairs, through the taproom and outside into the sunlight, where Raymond was waiting. Her face was dry and set. Her father kissed her, but she made no response.

A crowd had gathered around the gallows now, and three militiamen, wearing blue coats and white sashes, kept pushing them back. On the other side of the field, across from the crowd and farther away from the gallows, half a dozen Quakers stood in a little group, their long dark coats and flat-brimmed hats giving them an odd, funereal appearance. The three of us, Raymond, Sally and myself, walked across the field and joined them. They greeted us quietly. I knew most of them by name and all of them by sight. Now, at the other side of the field, over a hundred people stood, mostly men, but with a good sprinkling of women and boys and girls, and there was a chatter of noise and excitement out of them.

Saxon, the undertaker, drove up with his high-walled wagon, which he used as a hearse, and he and his assistant took out a plain pine coffin which they carried over to the gallows. At this, the sound out of the crowd increased. I glanced at Sally. She did not avert her eyes, nor did her face change. The long hitching rail in front of the inn was now crowded with horses and wagons, and other wagons were staked or weighted at the edge of the Common. There were people there whom I had never seen before, who must have come a considerable distance to see the Hessian hanged, many of them well-dressed, and women in expensive silk, with umbrellas to shade themselves from the sun.

We stood there waiting for what felt like an eternity but which could not have been more than half an hour, the afternoon sun still high in the sky, and then, from behind the inn, there came the rattle of a trap drum. That would be old Seth Harkness, who had played his drum for every parade on the Ridge since the war began; and presently he came into sight, dressed in the brown and green uniform that his wife had sewed for him, and playing a mournful roll on the drum. He was followed by the hangman, who carried a black scarf in his hand as a mark of his trade, and after the hangman, a dozen militiamen, marching six and six on either side of the Hessian. And following them, Packenham and St. August and Hunt, walking side by side; and after them some boys who came as close as they dared.

The Hessian boy marched with his head upright, his pale hair blowing in the wind, his step firm and sure; and my heart went out to him as never before for his crazy, indomitable courage and the pathetic glory of being a Hessian soldier. His brief moment of life was ending almost before it began, and he could only justify his meaningless death to himself by being brave; and there came to my mind and my inner sight a memory of all the other boys I had seen who clutched their guns and went to kill or be killed because they must be brave.

He stood before the gallows now, and the crowd had lost its voice in the presence of death, and an almost terrifying stillness settled over the Common. Now Pastor Dorset came walking across from the church, his book in his hands, across the Common to where Hans Pohl stood with his arms tied behind his back, and Dorset came close to him and began to speak softly. Yet such was the stillness that here and there a word of the whispering plea could be made out—life everlasting, there is no death, I am the resurrection and the life— but it could not drive the sour smell of death away.

Then the boy climbed the ladder, the hangman holding him, for his hands were bound, and he shook his head wildly when the hangman tried to cover his eyes. Then the hangman put the rope around his neck, tightened it, and pushed him into the open pit.

Sally stood there, weeping, her eyes upon the place where the boy had been.

13

The Meetinghouse

THEY CUT DOWN THE BODY finally, and I pronounced the boy dead. Then the Quakers carried the coffin to Dorset's house, the crowd trailing after us and then drifting away. Ziporah Dorset took Sally into her parlor to comfort her as best she might; and with the pastor, we took the body into his kitchen and washed it and cleaned the boy's uniform as best we could. Dorset gave us a quilt to place under the body and a hammer and nails to close the coffin with.

"He can lie in the church, if you wish," Dorset told us. "Believe me, he can lie in the church."

"Let him lie in the meetinghouse, and they'll bring the body for burial tomorrow. It's better that way. The girl wants to sit with the body," I explained, not desiring to add to Dorset's inner destruction, "and her mother and father and others too, perhaps. They wouldn't feel easy in your church."

Then we carried the coffin out and placed it in Raymond's wagon, and the other Quakers went to their own horses. Sally came out of the house with Ziporah, and again she appeared to be quite herself, her face dry and controlled. I told Raymond I would see him at the meetinghouse, helped Sally up to the seat next to him, and then watched them drive off.

Dorset stood beside me. The two of us remained there for a minute or two, and then I explained that I must go to the inn, where I had left my horse.

"Would they take umbrage if I came to the meetinghouse?" he asked me.

"They do not appear to take umbrage at anything."

"Before, I could think of nothing that I could do, and now there seems to be so much that I could have done."

"We all feel that way, I suppose."

"Do you, Doctor Feversham?"

"Yes, I do."

"Thank you," he said. "You're very kind."

I walked across the Common to the inn. The Common was empty now, the gallows standing in naked ugliness. As I took the reins of my horse, Abraham Hunt came out of the inn, saw me and walked over to me. He was limping slightly from his gouty leg.

"Well, Feversham?" he challenged me.

I could think of nothing to say, nor was there anything that I desired to say. I looked at him without hate and without wonder, and I understood him. Then I mounted my horse and rode off.

It had been a long, long day, and still it was before twilight when I reached the meetinghouse, a small frame building, like a tiny church without a steeple, sitting off the road near the top of Peaceable Ridge. At least a dozen horses and wagons were already outside, and I could see others coming up the road behind me.

I went into the meetinghouse. I had never been inside before, although I had passed by it many times, and even knowing a little about these people, I was unprepared for its plainness. There was no cross, no ornamentation, no symbol to mark it as a Christian place, just a room with pine benches, perhaps seating space for about forty people, and a lectern at the front of the room. The coffin had been laid in the space behind the lectern, but not covered in any way, not with a single flower on it, but just the plain pine boards, so bare that I could not help but being a little affronted by it.

There were about twenty people in the place already, men, women, some boys and girls, and others were coming in and sitting down quietly. So far as I could see, no one was attempting to conduct any kind of a service or worship, nor did the people on the benches appear visibly to be in any kind of prayer. They simply sat quietly, eyes cast down and hands folded in their laps.

Sarah must have come from her home, with Jacob and the baby, which she held in her arms, and Raymond and Sally sat on the bench beside them. I sat down next to Raymond, who put his hand on my arm and said:

"Thank thee for coming here in our time of grief."

I sat there then as they did, feeling strangely lost and out of place among these people, finding no answers, no hopes, no hint of any grace that could touch me. I sat there thus until no more people came, until there were about thirty in the room, and from outside, the long, slanting rays of the low sun cutting through the windows. I sat there and stumbled among my own lost hopes and desires.

Then Raymond rose and walked up to the lectern and opened the Bible that lay there. He searched through the pages, peering close in the poor light, until he found what he wanted.

"I will read from the fourth chapter of Genesis," he said, and then he read, "And Cain talked with Abel his brother: and it came to pass, when they were in the field, that Cain rose up against Abel his brother, and slew him. And the Lord said unto Cain, Where is Abel thy brother? And he said, I know not: am I my brother's keeper?"

"I know not," he repeated, closing the book. "I am my brother's keeper, and yet I know not."

The moon rose as my horse took me home, a great, wide moon that shed its pale light all over the landscape. The day had been eternity, and I think that more than anything else in the world, I wished for the small, parboiled priest to be waiting for me, so that I might go down on my knees and beg him, "Father, hear my confession." Yet I knew that even if he were there, it would change nothing, that for me there was neither salvation nor damnation but only the purgatory wherein a stranger lives, knowing that he will always be a stranger, coming naked and going naked, and knowing no more at the moment of his death than he knew at the moment of his birth.